#7

ELLEN ELIZABETH HUNTER

Ellen Eliz Hunter

MURDER ON THE CAPE FEAR

Magnolia Mysteries

www.magnoliamysteries.com

Published by:
Magnolia Mysteries

This is a work of fiction.

ISBN 978-0-9755404-5-9

Cover and book design by Tim Doby
Cover photo by John W. Golden

Also by Ellen Elizabeth Hunter

Murder on the Ghost Walk

Murder on the Candlelight Tour

Murder at the Azalea Festival

Murder at Wrightsville Beach

Murder on the ICW

Visit Ellen's website,
www.ellenhunter.com
Or contact her at:
ellenelizabethhunter@earthlink.net

ACKNOWLEDGEMENTS

I have often puzzled over historians' obsession with the Civil War, that is, until I began my own research into the Blockade of Wilmington. One fascinating discovery lead to another. The most riveting accounts were those penned by the participants: River Pilots James Sprunt and Jim Billy Craig; Colonel William Lamb, Commander of Fort Fisher.

I owe a debt of gratitude to friends for ideas expressed in this book. Hugs to Beverly Tetterton, Special Collections Librarian, New Hanover County Library, for suggesting the central theme of the plot and for sparing me the embarrassment of many errors. Kisses to innkeeper Chuck Pennington, The Verandas Bed & Breakfast, for dreaming up Melanie's real estate weekend. A big thank you to Cathy Stanley for suggesting that I set a murder scene in her bookstore, Two Sisters Bookery.

Tom Belton, Military Curator of the North Carolina Museum of History, was always just an email click away and always had the answers. Thanks also to Marla Trobaugh for researching the origins of azaleas in the Southeast.

Books I read were *Chronicles of the Cape Fear River* by James Sprunt; *Fort Fisher, Fortress and Battles* by Colonel William Lamb; *Lifeline of the Confederacy, Blockade Running during the Civil War* by Stephen R. Wise; *Masters of the Shoals* by Jim McNeil; *Confederate Blockade Runner 1861–65* by Angus Konstam; *The Wilmington Campaign, Last Rays of Departing Hope* by Dr. Chris E. Fonvielle, Jr.; and *Cape Fear Adventure* by Diane Cobb Cashman.

Kudos to photographer John W. Golden for the beautiful cover photo of the Cape Fear River and Memorial Bridge. John's artful photographs of Wilmington scenes can be viewed at The Golden Gallery at the Cotton Exchange or on his website, www.johnwgolden.com.

My talented designer Tim Doby is a Godsend.

The yummy recipe for Orange Coconut Cookies was a gift from innkeeper and chef, Dennis Madsen, The Verandas Bed & Breakfast. As Aunt Ruby says, "You have to feed folks if you want them to buy books."

The screw steamer merchant ship *Gibraltar* ran the blockade from July 1863 until July 1864. On her first trip she delivered two 27 ton 12.75-inch Blakely rifled cannons. The last known report of the *Gibraltar* was dated July 10, 1864. Her ultimate fate remains a mystery.

I tried to get things right, and as always to be respectful of Wilmington, her citizens and history.

THE CAPE FEAR RIVER

Native Americans called the river the Sapona after the Sapona Indian settlements along its banks. To the Spanish it was the Rio Jordan. To the English, it was known, alternately, as the Charles, the Clarendon, and the Cape Fair. Someone once called it "The Golden River," and as Wilmington artist Claude Howell spoke fondly of the port city's golden light, I wonder if he might have been referring to how the golden hue of the river tints the air.

The Cape Fear River originates at Mermaid Point, at the confluence of the Deep River and the Haw River in Chatham County, just below Jordan Lake. It is 202 miles long. Before it reaches Wilmington, it is joined by the Black River and the northeast branch of the Cape Fear. Below Wilmington the river widens into an estuary where salt water and fresh water mingle, and the river flows alternately inland and outbound. About twenty-eight miles south of the port of Wilmington, the Cape Fear merges with the Atlantic at the treacherous Frying Pan Shoals.

The river is navigable as far north as Fayetteville through a series of locks and dams. The upper Cape Fear is home to kingfishers and osprey, blue heron, and bald eagles. Once, the riverbed flourished with beds of mussels which filtered the water and made it clean. Now, the mussels are gone, a casualty of fertilizer and effluent runoff.

At Carolina Beach, the Intracoastal Waterway flows into the Cape Fear through a manmade channel called Snow's Cut.

The river has, since Colonial times, been crucial to the commerce of North Carolina. At forty two feet deep, Wilmington is the state's largest port.

During the Civil War, the Cape Fear River was known as "the life-line of the Confederacy." Urgently needed cargo --- guns, munitions, clothing, food, and gold --- were shipped from England, either directly from Liverpool, or through the ports of Nassau and Bermuda.

At that time, there were two entrances into the Cape Fear River, Old Inlet on the west, and New Inlet on the east, enabling the blockade runners to elude the blockaders. Through which inlet would those adventurous pilots make their dash? New Inlet was protected by the big guns at Ft. Fisher. Old Inlet was protected by Ft. Caswell.

The lower river is a graveyard of sunken ships. It is said that between the two bridges at Wilmington lie the remains of as many as fifty vessels.

This book is dedicated to my son James,
the recreational diver.

The Winds and the Sea Sing

Their Requiem

And shall

For ever more.

Inscription, Smithville Burying Ground

1

"Why would anyone want to steal that battered old brief-case?" Aunt Ruby asked Binkie.

"Well, I put it right there behind my chair so the customers wouldn't trip over it and now it is gone," Binkie declared, seemingly flummoxed at the disappearance of his decades-old briefcase. "What else am I to think?"

With a gleam in her eye, Aunt Ruby confided to me, "He's always losing things, 'specially his spectacles which most times sit perched atop his blessed head. I don't know what that man would do without me."

"And you wouldn't have it any other way," I said, amused by the pair of them. They were in their seventies but so much in love you'd think they were teenagers. They had been child-hood sweethearts who had never married until they'd redis-covered each other just last year. Now they were grateful to be spending their golden years together as husband and wife.

Aunt Ruby is my deceased mother's older sister. Binkie is Benjamin Higgins, History Professor Emeritus at UNCW. With both our parents gone, Ruby and Binkie have stepped in to become family for Melanie and me. I am Ashley Wilkes, historic preservationist and old-house restorer. My sister Melanie Wilkes is Wilmington's star realtor. Our mama had been besotted by *Gone With the Wind*.

"Help him look for the briefcase," I told Aunt Ruby. "I'll clean up the refreshments."

Two hours earlier, I had arrived at the Cotton Exchange to find a crowd of people waiting to buy Binkie's latest book, *Lyrics and Lore of the Lower Cape Fear*. I had squeezed through the open door at Two Sisters Bookery just as he was telling a circle of fans, "The very words 'Cape of Fear' were enough to strike terror in the hearts of eighteenth and nineteenth century sailors. In those days before radar and sonar, the Cape Fear with its shifting shoals and treacherous sandbars was navigable by only the most skilled and experienced pilots. Even then, a ship might strike a sandbar, the hull would sustain damage, causing the ship to flood and eventually sink. The Cape Fear River and the waters off Ft. Fisher and Frying Pan Shoals are a graveyard for a hundred sunken ships."

Cathy Stanley, proprietor of the bookstore, was stationed inside the open doorway, greeting customers and directing them to the guest author's table where Binkie was holding forth and in his element. Cathy has an open friendly face that makes customers feel at home. Reading glasses on a ribbon adorned her neck like a favorite necklace. "He's been watching for you, Ashley," she told me in a hushed voice.

Arms wrapped in front of her chest — her customary pose — she smiled broadly as her gaze seized upon a group of tourists crossing Water Street from the Hilton. Business would be brisk today. This first Saturday in June was typical of the perfectly glorious weather that attracted visitors to our city. The sky was cloudless — the cerulean blue we North Carolinians call Carolina Blue. On the west side of the Hilton the mighty Cape Fear River flowed south to the Atlantic, sunbeams glittering on the ripples like handfuls of diamond dust.

"Where should I put these?" I asked, offering a platter of fragrant cookies. Everyone who knows me knows my culinary skills are miniscule but I am working to improve this and that morning had baked Orange Coconut cookies.

"There's a refreshment table at the back of the store," Cathy told me with the wave of a hand. "Your aunt Ruby is back there. She took charge of it the moment she arrived. Bless her heart, she brought her famous peach iced tea. I made lemonade. And Michelle baked chocolate chip cookies. Oh yum, yours smell divine. I must sample one later."

The recipe for Orange Coconut Cookies* had been created by Dennis Madsen, innkeeper and chef of The Verandas, a bed and breakfast just down the block from my house on Nun Street.

Cathy extended her friendly welcome to the tourists from the Hilton as I moved further inside the jumbled, cozy bookstore, a place as comfy as home.

I squeezed past displays of bestsellers and racks of greeting cards, DVDs, and pictures of guardian angels, and made my way to the rear of the store where Binkie was inscribing a book to Beverly Tetterton, the Special Collections Librarian at the library's North Carolina Room. A stack of new books sat on the table to his right, and under the table was a large box, flaps open.

Beverly looked up, saw me, and waved but as she stepped away from the table she stumbled on Binkie's briefcase and almost fell. Apologizing, he got up, picked up the briefcase and set it down in the corner under a book shelf where it would be out of the line of traffic.

Aunt Ruby took the plate of cookies from me and sniffed appreciatively. "I declare, Ashley, you're becoming a regular Paula Deen! These look scrumptious. And we surely do need them, this crowd is ravenous. You know what I always say: You have to feed folks if you want them to buy books."

We laughed. I slipped my arm around her slender waist. "I'm here to help," I said.

Beverly Tetterton sailed off with a friendly goodbye as Binkie looked up, spotted me, and motioned for me to draw near. "Can you believe this turn out, Ashley dear? It does my heart good to see so many of our townsfolk taking an interest in the history of this old port city."

His lively blue eyes sparkled with excitement and good cheer, and the hands that enfolded mine were worn with age. He was wearing his favorite summer sports jacket with soft khakis and brown suede Hush Puppies. Binkie has been a boxer all of his life and the sport has kept him hale and hearty. After my daddy died when I was a freshman at Parsons School of Design, Binkie stepped in to become a surrogate uncle to me. Not that anyone could replace my wonderful father, and Binkie never tried, settling instead for friendship and offering unconditional support in everything I undertook. He was particularly delighted about my upcoming marriage to my partner Jon.

"I'd better let you get to your fans," I said, "and help Aunt Ruby 'feed folks' as she likes to say." I rejoined Aunt Ruby and together we offered cookies and filled paper cups with lemonade or iced tea.

"Is Jon coming?" she asked.

"Jon and Cam went diving this morning but he promised to be here. He asked us to wait for him."

"And of course we shall," Aunt Ruby said. "I adore that man of yours."

I do too, I thought with a soft flutter of my heart. How often does a girl get to fall in love with her best friend, with a man who is truly special by every standard. And who is romantic and sexy too.

As I offered cold drinks and cookies, I surveyed the crowd: students and senior citizens, society matrons and store clerks. The store was mobbed. One of the firemen came, and a clerk I had seen behind the counter at the post office. These were people from all walks of life who shared a fascination with local history.

Cathy Stanley drew near. "I'm worried that we're going to run out of books," she confided.

"Sold out! Now wouldn't that be grand," Aunt Ruby cried, clasping her hands together prayer-like.

Cathy hurried off to the front door again, greeting more incoming customers. The crush around Binkie's table continued for two hours. Just when the activity slowed, another round of patrons would enter the bookshop. And a grateful Binkie greeted each of them warmly, answered questions, and signed books, even though it was well after four and the book signing was slated to end at four.

Where was Jon, I asked myself, and watched the door for him to enter. But then I got so busy serving tea and cookies, I lost track of time.

Finally, things got quiet. Binkie stood and stretched. "I think that about wraps it up. I wish Jon had made it. And Melanie," he said, disappointed. "Now where is my briefcase? I thought I put it right there in the corner. I'm getting so forgetful, I don't know what day of the week it is anymore."

With a puzzled expression, he scanned the corner behind him for a second time, then the floor under the table. "You'd think that briefcase of mine had grown legs and got up and walked away by itself. Ruby, my love, have you seen it?"

"You two search for it," I said. "I'll clean up here. I'll just take these pitchers back to the bathroom and empty them in the sink. I'll rinse them too so they won't get your car seat sticky."

I moved past the rack of greeting cards and went through the children's book section to a screen door that led to Cathy's storage room and a bathroom. Clever lady! She had lined the screen door with a lace panel which emitted light and air, yet effectively blocked the clutter that filled the tiny storage space to overflowing. Behind me I could hear Aunt Ruby telling Binkie, "Let's look around. It's got to be here somewhere. Go ask Cathy if she's seen it. Maybe she stowed it at the cash register for safe keeping. I'll check the area up by the sofa."

With a pitcher in each hand, I bumped the screen door with my hip. The storage room was dark although I remembered a bright light shining out earlier. I pushed the door again but it would not budge. Something was holding it fast. Book boxes, I assumed. I set both pitchers on a bookcase, then gave the screen door a firm shove with my free hands. Feeling it yield, I edged the door open wide enough to squeeze through. Cathy has too much stuff back here, I thought to myself as I lifted the pitchers and stepped into the gloomy storage room. Light from the bookstore filtered through the lace panel. Shelves and a filing cabinet formed a short narrow corridor that twisted around to the right to the bathroom.

On the right a tiny niche served as an office. I tripped over something on the floor and went reeling into a stack of boxes which mercifully broke my fall. What in the world? I set the pitchers down on top of the nearest box and fumbled around on the wall beside the screen door until I located the light switch. A bright white florescent light flickered to life on the ceiling. Looking down, my first thought was that I had found Binkie's briefcase.

The briefcase lay overturned under a landslide of papers. White papers covered the floor and the man who was sprawled beneath them. He was turned on his side, knees drawn up. I realized I must have shoved his legs when I pushed the screen door open. Papers from Binkie's briefcase were strewn about and plastered up against the boxes. One covered the man's face.

Clumsily I dropped to my knees by his side, gently shaking his shoulder. The movement caused the paper to fall away from his face, revealing a man a little older than I with eyes wide open. "Are you OK? Can you speak?"

He did not respond. He did not move. Was he unconscious? Injured? Had he tripped over a box and knocked himself out?

"Help! Somebody help us!" I shouted, not yet willing to leave his side, silently urging him to react, to blink his open eyes and focus them on me.

I leaned forward for a better look. He was perhaps in his mid-thirties, clean shaven, with light brown hair and brown eyes. He wore dress slacks and a boldly-patterned shirt. For a moment the bold pattern and the papers concealed the splotch of blood that had spread across his middle. As I pushed the papers aside, I saw that a knife had been thrust into his abdomen directly up and under his sternum. His right hand gripped the handle, looking almost as if he had stabbed himself.

2

"I can't erase the image of that dead man's eyes staring up at me," I said with a shudder.

"Have another glass of red wine, Ashley," Aunt Ruby advised. "It's good for the heart and it will buck up your spirits. Benjamin, fill Ashley's glass, please dear."

Binkie lifted the bottle of red Merlot off the table and refilled my glass. Aunt Ruby is the only one who calls him Benjamin. Ordinarily this makes me smile but at that moment I was still in shock.

We were sitting on the deck at Elijah's Restaurant, having taken refuge there after two hours of being interrogated by the police. Homicide Detective Diane Sherwood was the lead detective, a woman who has it in for me. She had partnered with my former husband, Nicholas Yost, when he was on the force. The self-satisfied glint she got in her eye when the technician's lumalite revealed blood on my knees gave away the personal animosity she felt toward me.

"Naturally there is blood on my knees!" I exclaimed. "I knelt down beside the victim. I was trying to help him."

"No blood on her hands," the teck told Diane. She tried

to conceal her disappointment but I had seen it.

Diane knows I am no killer, yet the victim's blood on my hands would have given her a good reason to make my life hell.

Finally, acknowledging we were public figures and known in the community, and that she was acquainted with us personally and knew where to find us, she had let us go.

But she had walked with me to my car. "What do you hear from Nick?" she asked.

"Nothing, Diane! I do not hear from Nick. We are in the process of getting a divorce. You know that. We have nothing to say to each other. We talk through lawyers."

I reached for the door handle, then turned. "You are free to pursue him now, Diane. I've always known that is why you harbor this personal dislike for me. So go after him. You have my blessing. And if you can get him to settle down, you are a better woman than I am, and my hat is off to you." I pantomimed the doffing of an imaginary hat.

Then I got into my hot car, slammed the door shut and blinked back tears. Her antagonism had been the last straw that broke my composure. Dead bodies were her stock in trade — not mine.

And then Jon appeared, and I forgot all about Diane. I jumped out of my car and flung myself into his open arms.

"I had a devil of a time getting through the police barricades," he said and his voice held the tremor of fear. "I knew you were at Two Sisters and the radio said a crime had been committed there. I was so worried."

He pulled back to study my face. "Thank God, you are all right. When I saw the emergency vehicles here and knew you were inside, I was frantic with fear." His arms tightened around me so that his mouth was right at my ear. "Now that we are finally together, I don't think I could live if anything happened to you."

I leaned back in his arms to look up into his handsome face. Jon is golden and fair, with warm brown eyes, and a wry sense of humor that shows in his expression. But there was no sign of humor then, only deep, deep concern.

We had gotten into our cars and followed Binkie and Aunt Ruby out of the lot and driven to Elijah's at Chandler's Wharf. At six-thirty, the lowering sun was still bright, but we had gathered under a large green umbrella and there was a breeze off the river. The air smelled like early summer, like new green trees, and cool water.

But Jon was still reeling with excitement, and I could not get the dead man's stare nor Detective Sherwood's treating me like a suspect out of my mind. I reached for his hand. "We're all here together and we're safe, and that is all that matters. But that man! Someone killed him. And why did he have Binkie's briefcase? We just can't figure that out. Binkie had never seen him before he showed up at the book signing."

And once again we resumed our speculation about how and why the dead man had stolen Binkie's briefcase. "What in heaven's name did he want with that old thing?" Aunt Ruby asked.

But despite our wild speculations, no one had an answer.

"Is anything missing from your briefcase?" Jon asked Binkie.

"How would he even know?" Aunt Ruby responded. "That briefcase seems to contain every document he has ever owned."

"Now, Ruby dearest, you know that isn't accurate," Binkie said, and moved closer to slip his arm around her shoulder. "She's just upset," he said to us. "The police are keeping the briefcase and all of the papers they retrieved for the time being. They want me to come in to the station tomorrow to examine it and its contents. I suspect they are checking it for blood. The crime scene technicians bagged it.

They can do so much with DNA these days. Maybe the killer got blood or epithelial — that is skin cells — on the briefcase. At any rate," he told Aunt Ruby, "you've got your wish and we'll be shopping for a new briefcase."

He was trying to lighten the mood but it didn't work. Aunt Ruby *was* upset. Weren't we all? Jon was coming down from an adrenalin-high when he'd thought I'd been injured — or worse. "Why were you late, Jon? You never said."

"Where is Melanie?" Aunt Ruby asked. "I though you said she was coming."

"Yes, where is Melanie?" Binkie asked. "I'm a bit miffed myself that she did not make it to my book signing."

"She's got those investors in town for the weekend and she's showing them real estate. She rented every room at the Riverwalk Inn for her clients." Once again I found myself apologizing for my sister and the heedless way she trounced on people's feelings. Supposedly she had turned over a new leaf. So much for that.

"When I called her, she said she'd be here at seven, right after she showed one of her prospects a house."

Actually what she had said was, "We're talking big money here, Ashley."

"Money can't replace family," I had responded, "and right now your family needs you. So get your fanny down here fast. Aunt Ruby and Binkie aren't getting any younger, you know, and things like this really frazzle them." Me too, I wanted to add.

I sipped red wine and felt it warm my insides and calm me.

When the waiter came, Jon ordered hot crab dip with garlic croutons for all of us. Food would restore us. Food is a blessing, a gift we give thanks for. I love food. I eat when I am upset. I eat when I am happy. When I am stressed. And all the times in between. Because of my fondness for food, I am always fighting the extra pounds. My work is more physically demanding than most careers, still I am not the one who climbs the ladder to repair the roof, or to install the rehab windows. My physical activity is limited to being everywhere on the site and taking long walks around the historic district.

Jon ordered an iced tea. "I'll be the designated driver," he said.

"Or we could just walk home," I chimed in.

"Care to share the seafood platter, my love?" Binkie asked Aunt Ruby. And she assented with a nod and a smile.

Things were getting back to normal.

"I'll have the seafood marinara," I told the waiter.

"Blackened mahi," Jon said.

"Oh, look, there's Melanie now. Yoo-hoo! Melanie, dear!" Aunt Ruby called and waved. To us she said, "I knew my darling girl wouldn't let us down despite how busy she is. You know, they just voted her Wilmington's top realtor again. I'm so proud of her I could bust. You too, Ashley."

I looked up to see my dazzling sister cross the deck to our table. Melanie is the prettiest woman on the Carolina Coast. At age thirty-four, she is as gorgeous as she was at twenty-one when she was crowned Miss North Carolina. She had on a white linen pantsuit that was tailored to perfection over a white lace cammie, and high heeled white sandals. With her bright auburn hair bouncing on her shoulders, she caused heads to turn. How does she manage it, I asked myself. Even at the end of a busy day, she looked stunning.

Jon got up to hold out a chair for her and she slipped into it, chattering a mile a minute. "Thanks, sweetie. I'm sorry to be late but I was out at Landfall showing houses to some retirees, then I had to drive back downtown to return my guests to their hotel. Then I got stood up by one of my investors. I waited and waited but he never showed. And supposedly he is looking for a historic house to convert into a bed and breakfast. With the new convention center coming, there will be a market for additional inns and B&Bs downtown. I thought I'd show him Captain Pettigrew's house." She gave me a wary glance out of the corner of her eye.

Captain Pettigrew's house was the house Jon and I were restoring. "That house is not for sale, Melanie. How can you be showing houses that are not on the market?"

Honestly, sometimes her ethics just amaze me. "Besides, what is there to see? The house is basically a wreck. You can't even go inside because sections of the floor are missing."

"Oh pish posh, Ashley," she said, reaching for my wine glass and helping herself to a sip. "Don't get your knickers in a knot. When Laura Gaston hears what that house will bring even in its present condition, she'll sell all right."

How had the conversation so quickly turned from a devastating murder to Melanie's latest real estate coup, I asked myself. We were all looking at her, puzzled. Surely, she had heard about the murder. Why, I had told her about it myself when I'd spoken to her on the cell phone.

She caught our astonished looks. "What?" she asked, then quickly got the message. "Oh, yes. How dreadful for you. Tell me what happened. Every detail. I get so involved with business I tend to block everything else out."

"Surely not," I said.

She grinned at me and gave me a light punch on the upper arm.

"And Binkie," she apologized prettily, "I tried to get to your book signing but that became impossible. You did save a book for me, didn't you? I do want to buy one. I love displaying books like yours on my coffee table. They look so interesting. And I'll read it too, of course."

"Melanie, calm down, for pity sakes," I said. "You're as hyper as a six year old. Here's what happened: a man was murdered at Two Sisters in that tiny storage room at the back of the store. I found him. Actually, I tripped over him." I went on to describe the scene to her. "And you can't believe how maliciously that Diane Sherwood treated me. Why, she was actually disappointed that I did not have blood on my hands."

"Oh, don't let her get to you, sis. She's just jealous. I've had to deal with jealous women all of my life. Just ignore her," Melanie advised.

"But here's the really strange part, Mel," I continued. "The dead man had stolen Binkie's briefcase. We just don't know what to make of that."

Melanie gave Binkie a calculating look of appraisal. I could see the wheels in her head turning. Melanie is bright and quick, and woe to anyone who thinks she is just another pretty face. "Obviously there was something in your briefcase that was worth stealing. And I'd say the person who killed the thief wanted it too. That is the only explanation for the papers being strewn about and the only scenario that makes sense. So Binkie, what did you have in your briefcase that was important?"

"Why, nothing, Melanie. Nothing that anyone would want to steal. My research papers. Some scribblings. Notes to myself for another book."

Aunt Ruby interrupted. "Didn't I see a FedEx truck drive up as I was putting the iced tea in the car?"

"Why yes, my love, you did. I forgot all about that. There was a delivery for me, a padded envelope that I had to sign for."

"And what did you do with it?" she asked him.

A light bulb seemed to go off in his head. "Oh my. I put it in my briefcase."

"So there," Melanie said smugly. "I'll bet that's it. Something was delivered to you. Someone knew about it and wanted whatever it was. Or perhaps the sender changed his mind and wanted the letter back. Don't people send you old documents, letters, photos?" Melanie asked. "They know you investigate those things."

"Why, yes, people do send me historical documents. But mostly they arrange to see me and show me what they have. To see if there is any interest on my part. But yes, Melanie, you have hit upon something. It was one of those white plastic padded envelopes. I had thought I'd open it this evening in my study. My bride likes for us to keep the house neat, and that means keeping my papers out of the parlor," he confided with pride. Having a bride to care about the state of his house made Binkie very, very happy.

"I didn't want to take the trouble of unlocking the door again so I just stuffed it into my briefcase to be opened later."

"Did you happen to notice the return address?" I asked.

Binkie grimaced and shook his head. "I may have glanced at it, but I don't recall where it came from, Ashley. I was in too much of a rush, distracted by the book signing."

"I knew I'd find you here." Cathy Stanley heaved a huge sigh and plopped down, out of breath, into the remaining empty chair.

"Cathy! What is going on with the investigation?" I asked.

"Let me get a drink first." She raised a hand to the waiter. "Start me off with a glass of sweet iced tea right away," she told him, "followed by a double martini. Make that two. Yes, I said two. After what I've been through, I deserve them."

When the waiter hurried away she told us, "The police have closed my store. I can't open tomorrow either. They are processing it as a crime scene. I don't know when the crime scene guys will let me back inside."

"Consider it a well-earned vacation," Jon said.

"This can't be good for business," Cathy said worriedly.

"Oh, but you're wrong," Melanie exclaimed. "Trust me. When you open, there will be long lines at the door."

The waiter placed the iced tea in front of Cathy and she took a long swallow. "Gosh, I was parched. All this excitement . . ." She lifted the frosty glass and pressed it to her forehead.

Then setting it back down, she said importantly, "They identified the dead man from his passport. He's not an American, he's a Brit. Hugh Mullins. That's what they said, Hugh Mullins from London."

"Hugh Mullins!" Melanie exclaimed. "Why, he's one of my investors. He's the man who stood me up and caused me to be late. So that's why he didn't show! Dear Lord. Poor Hugh."

3

On Sunday morning I put on a pretty print dress and sandals and walked up Third Street to St. James Episcopal Church. Jon was meeting me there, driving in from Wrightsville Beach, and I found him waiting for me in what we informally refer to as The Wilkes Family pew. Not officially ours, but the pew where generations of Wilkes family members have always sat and where a brass plaque on the back of the pew proclaims it is dedicated to several generations of departed Wilkes ancestors. From the rear of the sanctuary I caught sight of Jon's golden head bowed in prayer. He is preparing for confirmation, and will join the church on the Bishop's next visit. We will be married here in December, a Christmas wedding. Melanie is planning our double wedding — hers to Cameron Jordan and mine to Jon. Lucky us, we have found our princes charming.

Most Sundays Melanie joins me here in our pew but after the bombshell that Cathy Stanley dropped last night — that the murder victim was none other than Melanie's client — she had dashed off to rescue her investors and to salvage what she could of the real estate weekend.

After the service, as Jon and I walked from the sanctuary to Perry Hall, I filled him in. "Melanie called me late last night. She was frantic. Seems the police are focusing on her group of investors because the victim was one of them."

"Makes sense," Jon said, "that the murderer would be someone who knew Hugh Mullins. Perhaps someone who came here with him?"

"That is how the police must be seeing it," I said. "They are not permitting any of her investors to leave town until they've undergone a thorough background check, are investigated and cleared. In these days of phony IDs, the murderer could simply vanish. Why, just the other day one of the magistrates was telling me how complicated his job has become because of the proliferation of bogus ID cards that cannot be validated."

We strolled along in the shade of two enormous and ancient hemlock trees. With the purchase and demolition of the firehouse on Fourth and Dock streets, and the construction of Perry Hall on that site, St. James Parish now occupied an entire city block, from Third to Fourth streets, and Market to Dock.

"How does that involve Melanie?" Jon asked.

"She rented out Riverwalk Inn for her guests for the weekend only. Now those clients have nowhere to stay and they are insisting that Melanie find lodging for them and even pay for it."

"But aren't they rich?" Jon asked, opening the door to the fellowship hall for me. "Can't they pay for their own rooms?"

"She says they are loaded. Otherwise, they would not have been invited. But how do you think rich people stay rich? By holding onto their money and spending yours, that's how."

"I suppose they do have a point. It isn't their fault that they can't leave. They came to Wilmington at Melanie's invitation and she stands to make a tidy sum in commissions when they buy."

"Unless one of them is the murderer," I said.

All talk of murder ceased as we got caught up in a discussion of the Millennium Development Goals, a movement to eradicate global poverty and hunger. But I did get some curious stares from the parishioners. I have a reputation for discovering bodies. A reporter for the Wilmington *Star-News* refers to me in print as The Magnet for Murder.

"Aunt Ruby and Binkie have to go to police headquarters today to examine the contents of the briefcase," I told Jon as we approached his Escalade. "This is all too stressful for people their age and I worry about their health."

Jon held the door for me. "We'll be sure to keep a close watch on them. Why don't we take them out to dinner tonight, then we can sit out back in your garden and have a nightcap."

Jon always says the right thing. Lord, I love this man, I told myself again.

He drove to my house on Nun Street. I adore my street and my house. The street is shaded by towering old oaks and magnolias. My house was built during the reign of Queen Victoria when houses were designed in a hodge-podge of styles. Basically it is Queen Anne in style but with a square cupola and Roman arches above the windows which are influences from the Italian architect Palladio. I had it painted a soft blue gray with white sashes and red trim. Jon had helped me to restore it two years ago in time for the Candlelight tour. That was when we'd started working together, and the joint effort plus our commitment to authentic restoration had solidified the bonds of our friendship

My house has a plaque that identifies it as the Reverend Israel Barton House. The house had been built for the Quaker minister in 1860 and quickly became a station on the Underground Railroad. He'd had a secret room installed which he had utilized to shelter runaway slaves. Many good people had lived in my house, although for a time it had been misused as a brothel. Every old house has a secret, I believe. Mine had many secrets, and I seriously doubted that I had discovered them all.

"How about we change our clothes, grab a sandwich, and head over to Captain Pettigrew's house," Jon suggested.

"I'd like that scenario a whole lot better if you included snuggle time," I said and kissed his cheek

He slipped an arm around my waist as I unlocked the front door. "This is one man who has his priorities straight. Let me help you out of your dress and we'll lie down for a while before lunch. You look pretty in that dress, but you'll look absolutely ravishing without it!"

"And no one is better at ravishing me than you," I said with a giggle and took his hand to lead him up the stairs.

Captain Thomas Pettigrew's house faced east on Front Street. The back of the house overlooked the river and there were porches and a lower level garden tucked into the hillside above Chandler's Wharf. We surveyed the garden that was filled with construction equipment. Scaffolding covered the rear wall of the house. Exterior siding from the millworks had been delivered on Friday, and on Monday, Willie Hudson, our general contractor, and his crew would begin the work of replacing rotted siding.

"While you were at the Old Carolina Brick Works on Friday," I said, "I had a paint expert take scrapings from wood sections all over the house. He bagged and labeled them — just like a crime scene teckie — and took them to the lab. Next week we'll know exactly what colors were original to the house."

"Want to bet they'll be wild and exuberant. Victorian houses were painted in polychrome, and popularly referred to as Painted Ladies. People tend to believe that the Victorians went in for dark and dreary, but not so — they loved bold colors," Jon said.

I looked up at the crumbling chimneys. "How did things go at the brickworks? Are they going to be able to match our bricks?"

Jon grinned. I love his smile. For a moment I was lost in it, as pure joy passed from him to me. He is perfect for me, I thought. Why did it take me so long to recognize what everyone else had seen? *Because it takes time for a girl to mature into a woman, Ashley sweetheart,* I heard my father's voice say to me.

"Ashley, are you listening?" Jon asked. "You seem to be a million miles away."

"Oh, just thinking about how cute you are," I said with a smile. "Go on, you were telling me about the brickworks. See, I was listening."

"You should have seen that place, Ashley," he said enthusiastically. "They do everything by hand. Mix up the clay and water as if they were making bread dough, then the mixture gets formed into what they call slugs. Workers pick up the slugs and pitch them into the molds. That's why they are called hand thrown. The bricks then get stacked and are run through the kiln at 2000 degrees. The bottom layer gets dark because of direct flame. The bricks on top come out lighter and are more uniform in color. They can match any brick color we give them."

"That's good news because the bricks along the foundation are a softer shade than the chimney."

"I took samples. We'll get the right color. I have absolute faith in those guys," Jon said.

I started up the outside stairs that ran along the side of the house. "Let's check on the inside."

In the mid-nineteenth century, Captain Thomas Pettigrew had been a river pilot as a youth, crewed on merchant ships, then later Captained his own ship, the *Gibraltar*. In those days, river pilots and ship Captains liked to build their houses overlooking the waters they plied, and Pettigrew had built his home in Wilmington while others had built houses in Smithville, now Southport, or on Federal Point, now known as Carolina Beach. A seafaring man's house often sported a widow's walk on the roof so that his wife could pace atop the house as she anxiously scanned the waters for sight of her husband's ship. But Thomas Pettigrew did not have a wife. He had been young, twenty-two, when he built this house for his mother Jessica Pettigrew and his younger sister Lacey. He lived here with them between voyages out to sea.

Jon slipped a key ring out of his pocket and undid the lock on the front door plus the padlock. The door was not original to the house and would eventually be replaced with a period door if we could locate one, or a reproduction if we could not. The windows that fronted the street were boarded shut while the period window frames and mullions were being rehabbed. It was dreary inside but we got the work lights on and were able to scrutinize the front reception hall.

Missing was an ornate stair rail and banister that we'd removed so that they could be stripped of paint and refinished. That left an open staircase which was not in bad shape. Stairs have a way of holding up better than other sections of a house although there were a few loose risers and worn treads on this staircase that we'd have to repair.

The reception hall had a fireplace, just as my own house did, and this one had been covered over with wallboard but it had been easy to spot the ghost marks of the hearth and that led us to the discovery of the fireplace. A new hearth and firebox were being constructed and the mantelpiece had been sent to a cabinet maker for refinishing. The tile surround was

intact and needed only a good cleaning to reveal its beauty —
a job I planned to do myself.

Jon led the way down a narrow hallway to the parlor at
the rear of the house and I followed. "Lots of water damage
back here," he said, shaking his head. "You'd think people
would take better care of their homes."

"I know," I agreed, "but Laura told me the repairs were
simply too costly for her and her father while she was growing
up and then in medical school. After her father was forced to
move out and the house was empty, one of the sashes rotted
out which caused the window panes to loosen and fall into
the garden and the gaping holes let in rain."
Sections of rotten wood flooring under the windows at the
rear wall had been ripped up. "The millworks said they'd have
floor boards for us next week," I reported.

"That's good news," Jon said as he walked to the center
of the room. Instantly, there was a loud crashing noise as the
floor under his feet cracked and caved inward. He was vanish-
ing before my eyes! My resounding Noooooooooo! echoed
throughout the house. The man I loved was falling to his
death!

Then I saw that he had caught hold of a sound floor joist.
"Help! Get help!" he panted, out of breath.

I pulled my cell phone off my waist band and started to
dial when Jon shouted, "I can't hold on. I'm going to fall. Do
something, Ashley!"

I had to think of a way to save him. I wasn't strong
enough to pull him up. Frantically I scanned the room for
something to throw to him, for him to hang on to. Behind
me, just inside the doorway, stood a heap of odd items, things
we had found around the house but had not yet cleared out.
One item was a coil of rope that we were saving because of its
age, thinking it might have some historic value. Would it
even hold, I wondered as I raced to grab it up. It might be so
frayed and brittle it would break. But it was my only hope.

In a flash I uncoiled the rope as I gingerly stepped to the edge of flooring where Jon hung. I did not want the floor to break under me too. We'd both be goners. I got down on my hands and knees, then stretched out full length on the floor. I dangled my upper body over the edge.

"I'm going to tie this rope around you," I told Jon. His face was mere inches from mine. Sweat was pouring off him, his skin was red, and his expression was strained. How long could he hold on?

I managed to loop the rope around his torso directly under his arms. My daddy had taught me to sail at an early age so tying a sturdy knot is something I know how to do.

"Hurry, hurry," he gasped. "My hands are slipping. Oh, Ashley," he groaned.

I forced myself to focus not on his words or the hopelessness of our situation but on the job of tying a strong knot. Then I slithered backward to safer flooring, jumped up and dragged the rope to an exposed stud and wound it around the stud and tied it tight.

"OK, I've got you," I hollered to Jon. "You're tied, but don't let go. I don't know how strong that old rope is." Oh, Lord, please let the rope hold, I prayed as I dialed 911.

Quickly I explained the situation and gave the address to the dispatcher, then hunkered down as close to Jon as I dared while we waited for help to arrive. His hands gripped the joist and his knuckles had turned white with the strain, but the rope bore some of his weight so he didn't feel so desperate, only frightened. I spoke reassuring words to him. "They're not far, Jon. They'll be here in a minute. You won't fall. I'm not going to lose you. The rope's going to hold."

The drop beneath him to the lower level was about fifteen feet, a fall sufficient to cause serious injury and perhaps even his death. The space below us was filled with construction equipment and directly beneath him was the table saw

— a fall onto the blade was too gruesome to contemplate.

When I heard sirens approaching I ran out to meet the firemen and to lead them back to Jon, the love of my life, the man who was hanging on for dear life.

They sized up the situation in a flash. The fireman I recognized from Binkie's book signing grasped Jon's upper arms and stabilized him. "I won't let you fall, buddy," he said. One of the other firemen said to me, "Can you let me into that basement? We'll put a ladder up to him. That'll be safer than trying to hoist him up. We don't want to risk him falling on that equipment below."

While he carried a ladder, I raced ahead down the outside stairs with my own set of keys in hand. Quickly, I unlocked the lower level door. A third fireman followed, and in seconds they had pushed the table saw aside, set up a ladder, and climbed up to steady Jon. The fireman who was holding Jon's arms let go, then went to untie the rope. Then they assisted him down the ladder. I ran to his side and threw my arms around him. "Thank God you're safe," I cried and covered his face with kisses.

4

"You're sure this letter fell out of the coil of rope?" Jon asked.

We were back at my house after locking up the Captain's house. Tomorrow morning when the crew arrived, they would rip up what remained of the unsound floor.

"Yes, I'm sure it was in the rope," I replied.

"Where did the rope come from?" Jon asked. "I'm sure glad you saved it, wherever you found it."

"Remember that stash of old stuff we found in the cupboard under the stairs on the first floor? It was there. Most of that stuff was junk but there were some things I thought the Cape Fear Museum might like to take a look at. The rope was one of those items. It looked so old, and well — I know this sounds fanciful — but I thought it might have come from Captain Pettigrew's ship." I raised my eyebrows and shrugged. "You never know. Wouldn't it be great if it had come from one of the blockade runners?"

"Wherever it came from, I'm sure grateful to you for saving it. It saved my life." Jon poured himself a second glass of cognac. "But why would someone put a letter in a coil of rope?" he asked. "Beats me."

"Hiding it?" I guessed. "It seems like a hiding place a child might choose. And Laura told us the Captain had a young sister — Lacey." And then I said, "Well, Jon darling," and I smiled at him, "I can honestly say that today I tied one stud to another."

Jon crossed the room to me, shaking his head as if now he'd heard it all, but grinning broadly as he reached out to give me a rocking hug. "That is the most feeble attempt at a joke I've ever heard. Okay, I'm going to stretch out on this sofa and I want you to read the letter to me. If I start to snore, don't wake me. I've had a hard day."

"You and me both," I said. "You sure you don't want to see a doctor?"

"I'm fine. The paramedics said I was OK. I'm just a little sore. I'll let you rub my shoulders later," he said.

"Only if you'll rub mine. I'm a little sore myself, sport."

I settled into the comfiest arm chair in my red library. This was my favorite room in the house. An artist friend had hand-stenciled gold fleur-de-lis onto the red walls creating a tooled leather effect. Two years ago tragic events had taken place in this room. Melanie had urged me to give up on the house and sell it, but I had decided to stick with it, to alter its course. Since then I have filled the library with loved ones, with holiday celebrations, and merry parties, happiness to dispel and replace the evil deeds that had been commited here. It had worked. You can create your own happiness if you really want to. And as an added bonus, the value of my house had escalated.

I removed the letter from the envelope. Both were very old. The paper was dry and brittle. The tattered envelope had turned a sepia color, as if it had been soaked in weak tea, but the stain had come from age, and the ink had faded.

Carefully, I unfolded the pages. The papers threatened to tear at the creases so I handled them tenderly. I looked at the last page first. "Oh, it's from Thomas Pettigrew himself. It is signed 'Your loving son, Thomas.' How exciting, Jon!"

I reshuffled the pages. "Okay, here goes. It's dated Christmas 1861 and the return address is Wilmington. "*Dearest Mother,*" he begins.

I have placed this letter in the hands of a trusted courier with instructions that he deliver it to you at your hotel in Washington. How like you, Mother, to disregard your own safety to travel into the fold of the enemy to give comfort to your girlhood friend from Maryland, Rose O'Neal. Everyone I talk to is appalled that Mr. Pinkerton had the audacity to place Mrs. Greenhow under house arrest. She has become a symbol and a martyr of the cause. Your visits must brighten her days as your presence here in our empty home would brighten mine. As much as I miss you and Lacey, my disappointment is insignificant when compared to your loyalty to your friend. How valiant Mrs. Greenhow must be as she awaits her hearing on a charge of espionage.

Little Lacey spoke only of you when I visited her at Aunt Martha's home. You will be relieved to learn that Lacey is happy in the country, treating the livestock like family pets. Her sweet face warmed the wintry day for me and I carry her visage in my heart.

Thankfully, I have my mates here in town with me for solace and to accompany me to services at St. James Church for the Christmas celebrations. Merry Christmas, dearest Mother. May God keep you safe and protect you as you abide in the land of the foe.

> *Your loving son,*
> *Thomas*

"What a sweet letter. Captain Pettigrew writes as if he had a classical education, don't you think, Jon? Jon?" He was sound asleep. I smiled to myself and was about to get up to fill my goblet when the doorbell sounded. The doorbell in my house is the old-fashioned type that you twist, and its harsh ring could wake the dead, but it is authentic to the house and I have not been tempted to replace it even for a sweeter sound.

Jon jerked awake, letting out a groan.

"I'll get it," I said. "You stay here and rest. We're not expecting Binkie and Aunt Ruby until six."

I left the library and went down the hallway to my front reception hall just as the doorbell shrilled again. I flung the door open wide to find Melanie and two strangers standing on my porch.

Melanie looked distracted. And she was angry with someone for her beautiful yellow-green eyes were snapping and popping — spitting bullets. The look she gave me was bitter, yet she kept her voice well modulated and calm.

"Ashley, sweetie, may we come in. I want you to meet two very special people."

Her look clearly told me they were not special, but two big thorns in her side.

As I closed the front door behind all three, my spacious reception hall seemed suddenly too full. The "special" woman weighed enough for two special women. She must have been carrying an excess of one hundred and fifty pounds.

Instantly, I felt sympathy for her. Did she have a thyroid problem? I am constantly struggling with my weight. I know how hard it is to keep trim. Then I picked up on her attitude which was one of impatience and that the world — and I in particular — owed her something.

Her long gray hair was braided and coiled around the top of her head. She had a "man in the moon" face, round and pasty, with an upturned nose and slits for eyes. But the blue eyes that regarded me from within puffy folds were shrewd and knowing. I placed her age at about fifty-five to sixty. When young she was probably fair and blonde and pretty but she'd let herself go — big time.

She caught me staring and her eyes narrowed further until they were thin hostile slashes. She was not happy with me, and I did not know why. She didn't even know me.

"Ashley, this is Patsy Pogue."

I extended my hand to her and said hello, but instead of a handshake and a greeting all I got was a huffy glare. Who was this woman, and what did she want from me?

Melanie brushed imaginary hair off her forehead and fidgeted nervously. Now normally my sister is the most confident person you would ever want to meet, yet somehow this hostile woman had managed to rattle her.

"Shug, I know you know who Patsy is. We've just caught you by surprise, is all," she said.

To Patsy, she said, "Ashley has read all of your books. We both have. Why, Ashley is always saying, 'Patsy Pogue is North Carolina's best mystery writer.' Don't you, shug?" She gave me a poke in the ribs, jarring me into my role.

"Oh, yes, I always say that, Miss Pogue." What was this all about? Wait until I get you alone, Melanie Wilkes, I thought. Why have you brought these strangers here to my house?

Patsy Pogue? Oh, yes. Light dawned on marble head. That mystery writer from Charlotte.

"Won't you come in?" I heard myself say. No one had bothered to introduce me to the mousy little man who fidgeted in the background. "Jon and I were just relaxing in the library. Come on back."

"I'd rather go to my room first," Patsy Pogue said.
Her room? Now I was on full alert.

Patsy turned to the insignificant little man. "Jimmy, why in tarnation are you slouchin' about? Go out on that porch and git our bags."

How could this woman be a writer, I asked myself. She couldn't speak English.

I watched, stunned, as she marched over to the front door and flung it open so hard I thought she was going to yank it off the hinges. Then I saw the bags. There must have been ten of them, of various shapes and sizes stacked up on the front porch, as if my house had been mistaken for The Verandas Bed & Breakfast down the street. And there was a computer, too.

Patsy Pogue started for the stairs.

"I'll show you to the guest room," Melanie said. Her glance implored me not to say a word. As Patsy hustled up the staircase, Melanie whispered, "I'll explain later."

Then she was gone, her voice floating down the stairs, "Patsy, I just know you and Jimmy will be comfortable in Ashley's guest room. She's got it all fixed up with pretty magnolia stencils and antique furniture. Why, the antique rice bed belonged to our mother's ancestors and was made in Savannah — oh heavens, ages ago — when they really knew how to build furniture."

I threw my hands over my face, horrified. That beautiful four poster with its hand-carved sheaves of rice was a treasure that had been in our mother's family since before the War Between the States. Generations of Chastains had bedded in it and some had been born in it. And now that three hundred pound, self-important mystery writer was going to smash it to smithereens!

5

"What's going on?" Jon asked sleepily. His golden blonde hair was tousled and his eyelids were droopy. I love his bed-head look. Made me want to take him upstairs, toss Patsy and her wimpy husband out of the second floor window, and get into the rice bed myself. But not alone — with this handsome, good man I was lucky enough to have fall in love with me.

"Doggone if I know. Melanie brought a mystery writer and her husband in here along with enough luggage for ten people and right now they are getting settled in my guest room!"

Thumps sounded from the floor above us, rattling the floor joists.

"Sounds like an elephant up there," Jon commented.

"She is," I declared. I could feel my blood pressure climbing. "Must be a glandular problem."

"More likely, a bar-be-que problem," Jon said.

Just then Melanie traipsed down the stairs. "Come on," she said sheepishly, and gathered us to her. "In the library. I'll tell you everything."

Arms crossed on my chest in my most belligerent stance, I posed in front of the mantelpiece. "OK, Melanie, what is going on? Why did you bring that woman here?"

Melanie collapsed in the leather sofa and buried her face in her hands. Then she wound strands of auburn hair through her fingers and pulled. She straightened up. She could scarcely look me in the eyes. "She's one of my investors and the police won't let her leave town even if she is famous. They are checking fingerprints and clothing for blood. So until they give the all clear, I am stuck with Patsy Pogue. She refuses to leave the historic district. The Riverwalk Inn had reservations for other guests so she couldn't stay there. I called every hotel and bed and breakfast in the district, and there's not a single room available. It's the height of the tourist season."

She gave me a pleading look. "Can't you put her up? Just for a few days? The police will clear her soon. She is a lot of things, but she is no murderer."

"Why can't she stay at your house?" I asked, indignant.

"I'd put her up but she refuses. She insists on staying downtown. Something about 'pickin'."

"What?"

"Don't ask me," Melanie replied, still pulling on her hair.

Gently, I drew her hands away. "Stop that," I said. "You're going to pull out your pretty hair."

"Oh," Melanie wailed, "she's driving me to distraction."

"Well, I won't have her driving Ashley to distraction," Jon said. "She is not Ashley's problem."

"I know and I'm so sorry to impose. I'll make it up to you, Ashley sweetie. I promise." She looked so contrite I knew I couldn't say no.

Instead I asked, "But why do the police suspect her. I didn't even see her at Two Sisters yesterday and surely I would have noticed. Did anyone see her there? She's supposed to be famous. Cathy would surely have recognized her if she came in."

"Well, it's not just her, it's Jimmy too," Melanie said.

"Yes, one does tend to overlook him, doesn't one?" I commented. "Do they have an alibi?"

"Oh, how do I know?" Melanie cried. "The police do not take me into their confidence. And you can see how difficult Patsy is. All she said was that they had been out pickin'.'"

"She could not have murdered that man," I said with certainty. "There was scarcely enough space in Cathy's storage room for me to maneuver through. Patsy would never have fit."

"But Jimmy is skin and bones," Melanie said plaintively.

"Ooooh," I said, understanding "The police may suspect him."

"And you thought you'd bring a murder suspect into Ashley's house!" Jon said hotly.

Melanie waved him off. "Oh, pish posh. Jimmy's no murderer. He doesn't have the ba . . . nerve to commit murder."

I rolled my eyes heavenward, up to the ceiling where the thumps continued. "Well, here is something I don't understand. Did you hear how that woman mangles the English language? How in the world can she be a top writer? She's published what? A dozen books?"

Melanie shook her head. "She dictates into a tape recorder and some poor assistant has to make sense of her ramblings and turn them into proper English. A ghost writer? Isn't that what they are called? Besides, most of the characters she writes about speak like she does. Uneducated, ignorant white trash. She writes about the most lurid crimes."

"You know I think I read one of her early books. Didn't she get an award?"

"Yes," Melanie replied, "and she's been riding that coattail for decades."

"She writes about a free-lance journalist, doesn't she? A woman who travels around the state writing about murders that happen all over. Fiction, as I remember. Correct?" I asked.

"Yes," Melanie said. "The crimes she writes about are fictionalized but sometimes based on true crimes. For some reason I'll never understand she can get people to open up to her and tell her things."

"But Melanie, what a poor impression readers outside of our state must get about North Carolina when they read her books. I remember that first one, and everyone in it was a redneck, as if she glorified ignorance. People must think that if we North Carolinians manage to finish seventh grade that is an achievement. When the truth is the Research Triangle area has more Ph.D.s than almost anywhere. And our cities are most cosmopolitan with outstanding museums and symphonies. What an insulting portrayal of our state!"

I love my state and I detest anyone demeaning it.

"Oh, what do I know about publishing?" Melanie cried. She was really beside herself. "Maybe that is how New York editors see the South and want to have it depicted. But I will tell you one thing, that woman has got money, and she claims she wants to buy a house here, so I've got to be nice to her. Please let her stay, shug."

"But what about your other investors? Where are they staying?" I asked.

"Most are prominent people, above reproach, who were cleared immediately and allowed to return home. One couple, Bo and Candy Murray from Greensboro are here on vacation and are staying with friends at Southport. My only problem guests are the Pogues."

Jon, who had been silent while we were having this little literary discussion about the merits and demerits of "barb wire fiction" shushed us. "She's coming!" he warned.

And sure enough the clomping on the stairs was heavy enough to make my poor old house vibrate with displeasure.

"Jon, would you whip up a pitcher of those mint julep martinis of yours," I asked. "I need fortification."

"Sure," he said, leaving for the kitchen. "I can see this is going to be one of those nights."

Patsy Pogue stomped into the room, her meek little husband following along meekly behind her. He *was* quite thin, I perceived, skin and bones as Melanie had described. He could have fit easily into Cathy's storeroom. A nursery rhyme flowed through my brain: Jack Sprat could eat no fat. His wife could eat no lean. And so between them both, they licked the platter clean.

I hoped the platters licked clean would not be my platters. Surely, they would have the good manners to go to restaurants for their meals and were not planning on me feeding them. I still had not agreed to let them stay. I was about to offer them a seat and a drink when Patsy blurted out ungraciously, "That guest room of yours was tee-nine-sey so I got Jimmy to move our things into that big bedroom at the front of the house."

My bedroom? She had moved into my bedroom!

"But that's my room," I protested.

"Oh, don't worry none, hon," Patsy said, "Jimmy done moved your stuff out of the closet and into the guest room. He's a right good worker when he sets his mind to it. Now we gotta git goin'. Pickin' to do."

I was almost afraid to ask but curiosity got the best of me. "Pickin'?" I shook my head to clear it. "I mean picking?"

Patsy folded her dimpled fists on her ample hips and glared at me, not sure if I was insulting her, but suspicious.

"Yeah, pickin'. You folks ain't never heard of pickin'? We passed a house on Fourth Street where they cleared out a huge stack of junk from inside. Could be lots of valuable pieces in that pile. Why, Jimmy and me done furnished our house in Charlotte with pickins. Good stuff, too. Lots a nice things from the fifties. You can't go wrong with the fifties look. It's makin' a come back, ain't it, Jimmy?"

Before the peevish man could reply, Patsy charged past him and headed for the door. "Jimmy, what in tarnation you waitin' for? Come on a'for someone beats us to that stash!"

The front door slammed and the sidelights shook.

"Melanie!" I screamed at the top of my voice. "What have you done to me?"

6

No sooner had Melanie left — amid gushing reassurances that I was the best, and that she'd never forget my sacrifice, and that she'd make it up to me in spades — and no sooner had I got comfy and snuggly with Jon on the big leather sofa than the door bell rang, again.

"I'm going to hire a doorman," I said, recalling the officious New York City doormen with their epaulets and top hats that I had encountered when I'd been a student at Parsons School of Design. Those guys knew how to keep uninvited guests out.

I gave Jon a parting kiss and slid out of his arms. "Hold that thought," I said, although I was not referring to his cerebral organ.

My libido slid into freefall when I checked the front porch through the sidelight. Oh no, not her again. I opened the door reluctantly to admit Homicide Detective Diane Sherwood. She was dressed in her usual mannish suit but there was nothing masculine about Diane. She was a very feminine woman with fine curly chestnut hair that brushed her collar. She was sleek and firm, from working out I assumed. One of these days I had to take up exercise. But I was not that desperate, not yet. Jon and I shagged. That was exercise enough for me.

Diane was alone. Usually, she works with another detective. Was this an official visit? Apparently it was. "I came to tell you that you have been ruled out as a suspect. For now."

For now?

"Come on back, Diane," I said curtly. This woman took pleasure in gnawing on my last nerve. She has had the hots for my estranged husband Nick for years, yet had never acted on her attraction that I knew of, probably because Nick did not return her feverish, maidenly yearnings.

She said hello to Jon and sat down in a straight back chair. Always in control, I thought.

To Jon I said, "Diane says I've been ruled out as a suspect. Isn't that a relief?" What I wanted to do was let out was a sarcastic, whoop-tee-doo!

Jon arched his blonde brows and said grimly, "I never knew you were a suspect."

"Neither did I. Well, now we know I am not one anymore. Or let's see, for now." I turned a frosty gaze on Diane. "OK, Diane, what is this all about?"

"Forensics has cleared you unless something else turns up. Thought you would like to know. Your prints were not on the knife handle."

"Well, I could have told you that," I argued. "And as a matter of fact, I did."

She went on as if I hadn't spoken. "No blood traces on your hands. Only on your knees but you can't stab a person with your knees, so you're in the clear."

"Diane," I said from between clenched teeth, "how long have you known me? Are you telling me you were seriously considering me as a suspect?"

Diane remained cool under fire. She turned to Jon. "Where were you yesterday afternoon, Campbell?"

I threw up my hands. "Well, that does it? Where will this end? Why don't we drag Binkie and Aunt Ruby over here and you can grill them too. Let's see, Binkie saw someone stealing his fifty year old briefcase so he went berserk and stabbed the man to death!"

Diane just widened her eyes in a maddening way and waited me out.

But then her question reminded me that I did not know where Jon had been yesterday afternoon. "Jon, where were you? You never did tell me."

Jon sighed. "I was waiting for the right time to tell you. I was at the hospital with Cam while he was getting checked out. He doesn't want Melanie to know but there was a little problem with his diving equipment."

"What problem?" I wanted to know. Had Cameron Jordan been in danger? Had Jon?

Jon looked from me to Detective Sherwood.

"Go on," she said.

It was pretty obvious he did not want to discuss this with her, but really he had no choice. She was conducting a homicide investigation and asking him if he had an alibi for the time of the murder might be stupid, but it was well within her rights. He had to tell her.

"We were diving off Cam's boat near Ft. Fisher, looking for sunken ships. You know there are about 150 ships that went down along the North Carolina coast and many have not been recovered or even located. We were descending when Cam developed a problem with his air tube. I spotted bubbles coming from the tank or a hose seal. He panicked and started hyperventilating. By the time I got him back on board he had blacked out even though I'd shared my mouthpiece with him. It was a slow leak and he would have been fine if he hadn't panicked.

"Anyway, we've got back-up oxygen on the yacht and I administered that to him, then sailed us back into port, and drove him to the medical center to be checked out. He's OK. But he doesn't want Melanie to know about this. You know how she over reacts to things."

"Well, I would over react too. If it had been you," I said. My voice sounded strained: angry and fearful at the same time.

Diane intervened. "So you are saying that you and Cameron Jordan are each other's alibis. I'll have to talk to him. How long was he unconscious?" she asked.

"Not long," Jon said hotly. "That is, not long enough for me to sail back to port, drive downtown to the Cotton Exchange, stab a guy I'd never heard of, and then retrace my steps and sail back out into open waters! If," he said sarcastically, "that is what you are suggesting."

"Not at all," Diane said mildly while giving us a smug smile as she rose out of the chair. "I wasn't suggesting anything. Just merely asking the obvious questions." She started for the library door, then turned abruptly, as if she'd had an afterthought. "By the way, I wonder if you've heard the latest. Nick has contacted the Captain and asked for his old job back. Guess the role of war hero slash adventurer has lost its allure. Thought you'd both want to know." And she stressed the word both.

Did she think Jon would feel threatened? She wasn't a good judge of character if that was what she was assuming.

I followed her to my front door, having to walk fast to catch up. I opened it for her and gave her a smug smile of my own. "Well, now you've got a second chance to snag Nick, Diane." As she stepped out, I called to her, "Don't blow it."

I returned to the library just steaming. Jon's face was flushed with suppressed fury. "Let's get out of here, drive out to my house. You're staying with me tonight. I need some peace and quiet and I need you all to myself, without Melanie and Patsy and Jimmy, and horny homicide detectives spoiling things for us."

I picked up Captain Pettigrew's letter, slipped it into my purse, and followed Jon out. I didn't have to pack an overnight bag, I kept clothes and toiletries at Jon's. I locked the door securely behind me. Patsy and Jimmy wouldn't be able to get in, but that was Melanie's problem, and I have to confess I just didn't care. I was with Jon. We needed a bit of peace and quiet. There hadn't even been time to tell Melanie about Jon's accident at the Captain's house.

On the drive to Wrightsville Beach, I called Binkie. "Change of plans. We're having dinner at Jon's. Can you drive out?" When he accepted with pleasure, I said, "Good. We'll stop for fresh catch and grill out on the deck. I have something to show you."

"Now this is what I call heaven," I told Jon, Binkie, and Aunt Ruby. We were sitting on Jon's deck, the fragrant smell of mesquite smoke wafting off the grill. Jon lives in a salmon pink house that backs up to the Intracoastal Waterway on the north end of Wrightsville Beach. The house is built on pilings sunk in the sand and the deck extends a few feet out over the water so you feel like you are floating. From a nest in tall grasses, a white egret watched us warily.

I love Jon's house; it is sparse and clean, uncluttered, with high-gloss wood floors that feel smooth and warm under my bare feet and are wonderful for dancing. His furniture was selected with an eye for comfort, everything capacious and deeply padded, his bed oversized and designed by someone who knew people did more than sleep in their beds. That thought brightened my spirits and I looked forward to bedtime.

I was sprawled in the lounge while Jon manned the grill. Binkie and Aunt Ruby looked relax and had a glow about them. I wondered about their love life. Do people in their seventies still make love? I looked at the two of them, so happy together, and thought: I sure hope so.

"What happened at the police station?" I asked them.

Aunt Ruby answered, "They're keeping the briefcase and all the contents. They had his papers spread out on a table but wouldn't let him touch a single document. Just wanted to know if anything was missing."

Jon turned from the grill. "And was anything missing?"

Binkie frowned. "Only one thing that I'm sure of. I don't recall every piece of paper that was in that briefcase. Would anyone?"

"But what about the envelope that you said FedEx had delivered just as you were leaving your house to go to Two Sisters?" I asked.

Binkie nodded. "That is the only item I can positively say was not there. A large white plastic padded envelope. Gone!"

I leaned back in the lounge. "So the murderer took it. That is what he wanted. What a shame we don't know what it contained."

"Oh, but I do know what it contained," Binkie said.

"Well, what?" Jon and I asked together.

"A journal. A very old journal. We got to Two Sisters a little early yesterday. I had no idea so many people would attend. I thought I'd be sitting there, whiling away time. So I opened the envelope and removed the contents. When I saw it was a journal, I though I'd keep it with me and peruse it during lulls in the book signing. I shoved the envelope back into the briefcase, and that is when my first guest, Beverly Tetterton, appeared. After that, we were busy, as you know, and I completely forgot about the journal."

"Where is it?" I almost shouted. "If I am right, someone wanted that journal badly enough to kill for it. Somehow he knew about the envelope and he grabbed that, possibly not knowing it had been opened. The envelope was padded, you say? He might not have known the difference."

Binkie grinned. "Yes, the flap was that self-stick kind so that it resealed itself as I was handling it. I placed the journal on a nearby book shelf with other books. And since Two Sisters has been sealed by the police until further notice, I am assuming the journal is still securely locked inside the bookstore. The police would have assumed it was part of the stock, if they even noticed it."

Aunt Ruby leaned forward. "We'll call Cathy Stanley and ask her to let us know the minute the police permit her to reopen. Then we will all hurry over there and collect that journal. I, for one, want to see what it contains."

"So do I," I said.

"Now wait a minute," Jon said. "That might be dangerous. We ought to turn it over to the police."

"Not without examining it first," Binkie said. "It was sent to me and I want a good look at it before I release it to anyone."

"Do you happen to remember the return address?" I asked.

Binkie looked bewildered. "I do not remember. I do recall clearly that I had to sign for it. But people often send me historic documents to examine. That is not unusual. Oh, wait a minute, it might have been from New York."

Jon said thoughtfully, "But I'll bet no one has been killed for one of those historic documents."

"That's where you are wrong," Binkie said.

Jon raised the lid on the grill. "Fire's ready. Nice hot ashes." And he lifted grouper fillets with tongs and set them on the grill.

I reached for my iced tea, and said, "Speaking of historic documents, I have a treasure for you, Binkie." And I handed him Captain Pettigrew's letter. "He wrote it to his mother when she was in Washington, visiting Rose Greenhow who was under house arrest for espionage."

As Binkie examined the pages, I gazed out over the waterway. It was that peaceful time of evening when folks were preparing their dinners or dressing to go out. Few powerboats cruised the waterway. Waterfowl had reclaimed the marshes in their absence. The setting sun painted the golden marshes a color that was almost coral. And the water shimmered with reddish-gold highlights.

Binkie handled the pages as carefully as I had. "This is indeed valuable. You must turn it over to the Cape Fear Museum or to the library's archives. Give it to Beverly Tetterton, she'll know what to do with it. Their collection includes a few letters from Captain Pettigrew, and I know they will welcome this addition. Do you suppose there are any others tucked away somewhere in the Captain's house?"

"Great minds," I said with a laugh. "I was thinking the same thing. Captain Pettigrew had a little sister named Lacey. He refers to her in the letter. I think it was she who hid this letter in the back of the cupboard, tucked it inside a coil of rope for safekeeping. It's something a child would do. And it has been there for a century and a half."

Jon turned, tongs in hand. "The grouper is ready. Another minute for the vegetables." He plated the grouper on a large serving platter and set it on the grill's cover to keep it warm.

"I've seen the plaque to Rose Greenhow on Third Street countless times so I know she was buried at Oakdale Cemetery with full military honors, but how was it that she died in Wilmington?"

"The tale of Mrs. Greenhow's adventures and tragic death are stranger than fiction," Binkie replied. "From house arrest, Mr. Pinkerton transferred her to the Old Capitol Prison. But Mrs. Greenhow had friends in high places, extending to members of Lincoln's cabinet. She was said to have been a most attractive and charming hostess. Therefore, she was much too popular and incendiary a figure to be tried formally. A hearing was held during which she declared it was not her fault that men in positions of trust blathered freely into the ear of the first pretty woman they came upon. The judge basically washed his hands of the entire incident and banished her to Richmond.

"Later, Jefferson Davis enlisted her for a mission to England and France as a propagandist for the Southern cause. England's official position regarding our civil conflict was one of neutrality, but their textile mills were in desperate need of the South's cotton, thus motivating them to find ways to circumvent neutrality. English shipping companies were the owners of most of the blockade runners. It was in England's economic interest to ensure the free flow of trade."

It never ceased to amaze me how Binkie could make history sound as real as events of today. I hung on his every word, as did Jon. And Aunt Ruby gazed at him adoringly.

Binkie continued, "Mrs. Greenhow raised money for the Confederacy. She wrote a book about her imprisonment and was able to raise $2,000 in gold from the proceeds of its sale. She boarded the *Condor* for her return trip home. Approaching the Cape Fear, the *Condor* ran the outer line of blockaders, but as she neared the bar at New Inlet, she was chased by the Union gunboat *Niphon*. In attempting to avoid a collision with a grounded blockade runner, Captain Hewett turned to starboard and found his ship grounded, as well.

"Mrs. Greenhow was fearful of being captured by Union forces, and rightly so, for she was carrying intelligence dispatches addressed to President Davis and she would have been imprisoned again. She persuaded the Captain to launch a small boat to take her ashore. But the small boat capsized and Mrs. Greenhow drowned, weighed down by the pouch of gold sovereigns she wore around her neck."

"Dear, dear, what a tragedy," Aunt Ruby murmured.

"Her body was washed ashore at Ft. Fisher, where she was recognized and delivered to Wilmington for a full military burial."

"What happened to the gold?" Jon wanted to know.

"It is said a sentry delivered the gold to Colonel Lamb, but there is no reference to this occurring in Colonel Lamb's writings."

"Perhaps the pouch opened and the gold sovereigns spilled out and sank to the bottom of New Inlet," Jon speculated.

"If that is indeed what happened to the gold," Binkie said, "we shall never know. In 1872 the Army Corps of Engineers closed New Inlet by constructing a rock dam with granite capstones."

Jon opened the grill and added the vegetables to the platter. "Still, I wonder what a gold sovereign is worth . . ."

His words were cut off by the roar of a speed boat. A white boat cut straight across the waterway and bounced over the current. Pelicans flew up and out of the way with squalls of protest. The boat was flying straight at us, on a collision course with our deck.

"Up!" I shouted. "Run! In the house."

"What?" Aunt Ruby cried, turning. I grabbed her arm and propelled her inside. Binkie followed. Jon rushed in behind us and quickly slammed the French doors shut.

We all stared out through the glass panes, horrified. Would the pilot be able to stop in time? Was his boat out of control? Just as he was about to crash into the rushes which would have choked his propellers, the boat turned sharply and veered away from the shore so fast it almost overturned. A great plume of water sprayed up behind the boat. The lone pilot had almost crashed into the deck. It had all happened very fast, but I had a distinct impression of a man in a ball cap and a tent-like shirt, training a pair of binoculars on us.

7

Willie Hudson was angry. He balled up his fists and gave the door a fierce look, like it had ruined his morning. Willie, who is our general contractor and who knows more about old house construction than Jon and I put together, is normally the epitome of laid back. But not on this Monday morning. Not as he surveyed the wreckage of Binkie's front door.

"Well, at least they didn't get in," he said stonily. Then, shaking his head negatively, he said, "Sometimes, I think I'm getting too old for this world. Too much crime in the world today. Too much senseless crime. Why, you can just look at the professor's modest house and know he doesn't have plasma TVs in there. Nothing worth stealing, unless you're into history books."

Last night after we had recovered from the speed boat's near miss of Jon's deck, we had gone on to enjoy a pleasant dinner of grilled grouper and grilled veggies. Then Binkie and Aunt Ruby had returned to Binkie's house on Front Street to find that someone had tried to break the lock and pry the front door open. When the housebreaker had not gained entry through the front door, he had gone around back and tried the same thing on the back door. The back door had yielded, but then the burglar had found himself inside an enclosed kitchen porch and prevented from entering the house by a second solid door.

Binkie was no fool. He and Aunt Ruby divided their time between his Wilmington house and her house in Savannah. Binkie had seen to it that both houses were secure in their absence. He had not installed an alarm system because they could be super-sensitive, going off if the paperboy hit the door with a tossed newspaper and he would not be there to turn it off. But he had had Willie, our general contractor, install steel core doors and sturdy locks here at his house on Front Street.

"This door is so banged up, I think I'd better buy you a new one," Willie told Binkie. "I'll put it up for you, free of charge. The back door too. But the destruction to Ruby's crafts, well, that's just plain vandalism. All that pretty pottery, so lovingly hand-painted — tossed and broken on the floor, clay shards everywhere. It's a crying shame. That man was enraged. Mad as a wet hornet that he couldn't get in. I don't know why someone would go to so much trouble when there are bigger, richer homes all about."

His gaze traveled north to the Colonial-era Brown-Lord House on Front Street and Ann, with its pink painted exterior and white sawn work and a history that went back to before the American Revolution. The handsome Italianate Honnet House was just a few doors south, and on the next block there was the magnificent Governor Dudley Mansion. Willie was right to wonder why a burglar had selected Binkie's modest home.

But Jon and I knew. We exchanged knowing glances. The journal — he was after the journal. But it wasn't here. It was still at Two Sisters. I couldn't wait until we could get our hands on that journal to see what was so valuable about it that someone would kill for it, and then attempt this break in.

Binkie looked defeated. The past two days had taken their toll on him. Aunt Ruby was lying down upstairs, a cold pack on her forehead. Poor dears.

Binkie shook hands with Willie. "I'd appreciate it if you'd take care of everything. If you'll buy new doors and get them installed as quickly as possible, my bride will sleep better."

"Does Aunt Ruby want to return to Savannah?" I asked. "I'd understand if she wanted to escape from this crime wave."

Binkie fixed me with a glum look. "Ashley, our lovely Belle of the Ball Savannah has become a tarnished lady. The poverty and crime rates in our beloved Savannah are now among the highest in the nation. We were waiting for the right time to tell you this, but Ruby is seriously thinking of donating the Chastain family home to the city to serve as a museum. They have the resources to maintain it and to safe-guard it from vandals.

"And as for our leaving Wilmington, well, that aunt of yours is feistier than the Queen of England. She said it's bad enough she's being driven out of one home — and she's smart enough to know when she's licked — but she's taking a stand in Wilmington. Said if she had to go out and buy a shotgun and sleep with it under our bed, she'd do it. She is my kind of woman."

Willie started for his truck. "Meet you at the Captain's house in a couple of hours," he said to Jon and me. "And Jon, I sure am sorry we failed to discover how bad that floor was. I just hate it that it collapsed under you and I'm relieved you were not hurt."

Then to Binkie he said, "I'll personally select the doors, and I'll have one of my grandsons install them for you." He gave me a pointed look. "Does all this have anything to do with that body you stumbled over on Saturday? I declare, Miz Wilkes, you sure have a knack for finding them dead bodies." Then he left, looking as disheartened as Binkie.

"I'm with Ruby," Binkie said. "I refuse to budge. Just as soon as Cathy Stanley opens her bookstore, we are retrieving that journal and we're going to read every word until we find out what this is all about."

"We'll work on it together," Jon said. "If anyone can decipher an old journal, it is you, Binkie. Ashley and I will help. And maybe we'll learn something that will lead us to the murderer. Then we'll turn the entire matter over to the police."

"That's the way I see it," Binkie agreed. "They were not very impressed with this attempted break-in when they came last night — practically yawned in my face. Nothing to report stolen, they said. They just filed a report, attempted break-in. Plenty of those, they said. Now if you'll excuse me, I think I'd better lie down for a little while."

Jon and I strolled up Front street toward Captain Pettigrew's house. The morning air was soft as a whisper, another beautiful June day. Magnolias bloomed all over town, their fresh lemony smell sweetening the city streets.

"If it's gotten as bad in Savannah as Binkie says, I don't want them staying there," I told Jon. "The city was going downhill when I did my graduate work there at the Savannah College of Art and Design. Old families like mine, struggling to hold onto their homes in the face of so much general poverty. It's such a contradiction. There are those lovely, spacious old homes, and all around them people are living in the streets."

"The gap between the rich and the poor just gets broader and broader," Jon said.

"But not everyone who owns a historic house is rich," I said. "Some of us, like Aunt Ruby and clients like Laura Gaston are caught in the middle, doing their best to hold onto their heritage."

Jon gave me a hug. "Don't let this get you down, baby. I think Ruby's solution is the best. Donating the Chastain home to Savannah only benefits that city. And on the plus side, we get to have Binkie and Ruby here with us year round."

I gave him a quick peck on the cheek. "Thanks for helping me to put this in perspective. And speaking of vandals, and Goths and Visigoths, guess I'd better check on my own Vandals when we break for lunch," I said.

Hand in hand, we continued toward the Captain's house where the noise of hammering created a mighty din. Carpenters on scaffolding were replacing the bad siding with new, while a second crew had removed the plywood and were installing the rehabbed windows. I stopped at my van to get my hardhat out of the backseat and Jon stopped for his. Our heads protected in bright yellow hardhats we stepped under the scaffolding and through the front door which was wide open. Immediately, we bumped into Jimmy Pogue in the reception hall.

"What are you doing with those boxes?" I screeched. Jimmy was carrying out the boxes of historic artifacts that I had earmarked for the museum. "Put them down now!"

"You are not allowed in here," Jon said, as indignant as I. "This is a restricted area. We've got liability here. You've got to leave."

"No sir, you're wrong," Patsy shouted from the stairs which, without a stair rail to hold onto, she descended precariously.

I expected to see her fall at any moment. Her legs were stuffed into a pair of tight jeans so that they looked like two Smithfield sausage links, and she was having difficulty bending her knees with each downward step.

But her mouth was functioning super fine. "Melanie said this house is for sale and that includes the contents. And I done told her I intend to buy it and everything in it!"

I exploded. "Melanie is wrong and you are wrong, and if you don't leave at once I'll have you escorted out of here!"

"And put down those boxes!" Jon yelled at Jimmy.

Jimmy dropped the boxes like they were the burning bush.

He didn't say a word, just twitched a bit as we stared him down. Was he mute? It occurred to me I had not heard him utter a single word since we met.

But Patsy had no trouble speaking. "I have a bone to pick with you, missy."

Now what?

"You locked us out last evening. You went off with your lover here and didn't give a hoot as to how me and Jimmy would get back inside our room."

Her room?

"Lucky for us, we had our cell phone and we called Melanie. She had to drive all the way back into town to let us in. But at least she gave us her set of keys so we won't be locked out again."

I was speechless. But Jon said, "What do you hear from the police? When will they let you leave town?"

"We ain't in no hurry to go home, are we Jimmy?" But Jimmy was already showing us his back as he headed out, and if he replied I did not hear.

Patsy went on, "Pickins here is good, and I'm on to a sensational story. Got me a humdinger of a plot for my next book. Melanie is bringin' her boyfriend over tonight for dinner. I'm as good a cook as that Paula Deen any day. Anywho, he's a big TV producer and I'm gonna make my pitch to him for my own TV show."

She sashayed past us on her way out. "If you two got plans for tonight, don't feel like you have to come. I'll understand. No problem. I done figured out where all the pots and pans were stowed when I cooked us our breakfast this mornin'. You sure do keep a paltry refrigerator, missy. I had to send Jimmy out for bacon and eggs." She looked from me to Jon. "How'd you expect to keep a man if you ain't gonna feed him? Didn't your mama tell you the way to a man's heart is through his stomach?"

"Leave Ashley's mother out of this," Jon declared.

But Patsy ignored him, and pointing to the boxes filled with the Captain's artifacts, she said, "Don't you go givin' them pickins to nobody. They come with the house, and I'm buyin' this house. Check with Melanie! Whaddya think I drove down here for and why do you think I'm a'stayin'. Ain't because of them police. If I wanted to leave, I'd leave. I got me the best law firm in Charlotte on retainer to deal with annoyances like the police. And now that Mullins is out of the biddin', this house is mine."

At that point I lost it and stuck my face into hers. "For the last time, this house is not for sale!"

But my words didn't faze her. She stopped on the porch, her gaze fixed on the curb and the pile of trash we had cleared from the Captain's house. She turned to give me one of the defiant looks I was actually growing accustomed to. "Don't underestimate me, Missy. I won't born in no barn. That stuff out their waitin' for trash pickup is fair pickins. You can't stop me from goin' through that stash and takin' anything I damn well please!"

8

"You're looking fit as a fiddle," I told Binkie.

He beamed and let me into his house through the new front door. "Come on back and we'll give you the best bacon and tomato sandwich you've ever tasted," he invited. "I spent the morning at my favorite gym, beating the dickens out of a punching bag. If I find someone trying to break down my door again, watch out!" And he lifted his fists in his best pugilistic stance.

Binkie had been boxing since youth, and the exercise kept him in shape, for as a scholar he led a sedentary life style. Still I hoped he was not serious about tangling with a burglar; he was too old to be getting into fistfights. Unlike a punching bag, the burglar would hit back.

"I've got news. I know who sent the journal."

"Do tell! Join us for lunch and tell me all about it. My bride watches her waistline and mine too. Turkey bacon and nine grain bread and tomatoes from the garden."

And he led me through the house to the shady patio where Aunt Ruby welcomed me. I observed that the kitchen porch which Aunt Ruby used as a crafts room had been cleaned up and restored to its former self. "Sit right down here, Ashley dear," Aunt Ruby welcomed me graciously. She'd been working on her pottery, with paint smudges on her soft loose-fitting slacks and blouse. "Take my sandwich, dear," she said, "I haven't touched it yet. It's still warm. I'll just run inside and make another. But don't you dare share your news until I return."

She went into the kitchen, fetched a tall glass for my iced tea, then disappeared again.

"She's the boss," Binkie said proudly. "We won't discuss your news until she returns."

I helped myself to iced tea from the frosty pitcher.
"She sweetens it with honey," Binkie said. "That's why it's so good. I'm going to live to be a hundred with her watching out for me. You know she's a retired nurse," he said proudly. "She knows what's good for folks our age."

"Folks of any age," I said, and bit into the dense grainy bread. "Oh, yum, this is scrumptious. You know, Binkie, I think you have lured every bird in New Hanover County into your garden." There were bird feeders of various sizes, filled with a variety of seed, and a bird bath. Sunflowers grew at the far wall that separated Binkie's garden from his neighbor's property and mourning doves waddled along under them in hopes of a fallen seed.

Several hibiscuses were blooming a brilliant red. "The humming birds love those red flowers," Binkie said, drumming his fingertips impatiently on the patio table. He was eager to hear what I had to say.

"It's amazingly quiet out here," I said. From the street came the steady clip-clop of the Springbrook Farms horse and carriage as it carried tourists through the district.

"Yes, for downtown it is quiet, thanks to our abundant live oak trees and magnolias, and our many azalea bushes. The foliage absorbs noise."

In the background Memorial Bridge sang with traffic, a sound I was accustomed to and found soothing. There was intermittent street traffic. Then the quiet was obliterated by a fire truck roaring by, siren warbling.

When Aunt Ruby rejoined us with a plate of more sandwiches, I related my news, "I had a call from my client, Laura Gaston. We discussed the progress on the house, and she asked about the murder at Two Sisters. Seems we made the national news — a murder in a bookstore during a book signing, interest there — so she heard about it in New York."

"New York!" Binkie exclaimed. "That was the return address. She sent the journal!"

"She asked me if you had received it. She apologized for sending it by FedEx. She has begun packing for her move back to Wilmington but wanted to get the journal into your hands. And she's off to a medical convention."

"And did you tell her the journal might be the motive for the murder here?" Binkie asked.

"I did and she is as puzzled as we are. She has looked through the Captain's journal and can't believe someone would kill to get it. She said she had included a letter to you. Did you see a letter?"

"No," Binkie answered thoughtfully. "It must have remained in the envelope when I withdrew the journal."

"So whoever stole the envelope has the letter too and knows the journal was sent by Laura Gaston," Aunt Ruby said.

"I wonder if he didn't already know that," I speculated. "Otherwise, how would he have known about the delivery of the journal to Binkie?"

"Unless the dead man told him," Binkie said.

"But how did the dead man know?" I asked.

Binkie answered, "He must know Laura Gaston and knows that she had a journal in her possession that she was sending to me. And of course the journal had to have been written by Captain Pettigrew."

"Laura and her father are Captain Pettigrew's only living relatives. And her father has been in poor health for several years, ever since that hit and run accident."

"Oh, I remember that," Binkie exclaimed. "It happened right out there on Third as he was crossing the street. Traffic moves much too fast on that street. And the driver didn't stop and was never traced."

"Laura's father had been living in the Captain's house until the accident. Then he just couldn't manage in that large house alone. And Laura was in medical school at the time. Now he lives here in the historic district in a small apartment in a private residence. He's in a wheel chair and has to have nurses. He is why Laura became a surgeon, so she could help injured victims like her father. She has finished her surgical residency at New York University Hospital, and she's moving here to live in the Captain's house. She's engaged to a local man and she's already been asked to join a local surgical practice. Her father will move into the Captain's house with her after we've remodeled it. Jon and I are outfitting the first floor to meet the needs of a handicapped person."

"Tell me again how that lineage goes, Ashley," Aunt Ruby requested.

"Captain Pettigrew never married, so he had no direct descendants. He disappeared at the end of the Civil War and his family never knew what happened to him. They believed he went down with his ship because his ship was never heard of again either. Those last days of the war were chaotic."

"Laura Gaston is descended from the Captain's younger sister Lacey," Binkie said. "I've ascertained her genealogy. Lacey Pettigrew married Andrew Gaston, a young man she met after the war. Together they produced two sons: one died in childhood, the other grew to manhood, married and had a family."

I jumped in. "And sadly most of that family was wiped out during the great influenza pandemic of 1918. Few survived, until today Laura and her father are the last of that line. With his poor health he has transferred his interest in the house to Laura."

"Why, I declare," Aunt Ruby said, "it is amazing that the family managed to hold on to that house."

"For that we can thank Lacey Pettigrew. She had the foresight to set up a trust fund with the money Thomas had earned and saved and entrusted to his mother. The trust fund paid for the upkeep of the house and the taxes. She was determined that it remain in the family and as you can imagine that was difficult during Reconstruction. She herself lived in the house until she died, long after Andrew Gaston had passed on and her only surviving son had gone out into the world. Trustees have administered the trust ever since. The trust was almost broke until Laura's fiancé stepped in and provided the funds to pay last year's taxes. Vandals had been breaking into the house and the city was about to condemn the property. Laura persuaded them she would repair and restore the house, and she borrowed money based on her future earnings to do so."

"Amazing story," Aunt Ruby said. "Just shows how determined folks can be to hold on to their heritage."

"I can't wait to see how wonderful you make that house, Ashley," Binkie said. "You and Jon perform miracles. It will be the showplace of the community if I know anything."

"Thanks," I said. "You are both dears and I love you to death. Thanks for lunch and now I've got to run along home to check on my house and see if it is still standing or if that dreadful Patsy Pogue has had the house movers come and carry it off to Charlotte, another one of her 'pickins."

I walked south to the corner of Nun Street, then turned east toward Third. On the corner of Second and Nun stood the stately Verandas with its tiers of porches, front and back, one of two B&Bs in Wilmington to be chosen by Select Registry. Historically it had been Captain Benjamin Beery's house. Captain Beery had been a ship builder during the Civil War and had constructed a monitor atop the house from which lookout he spied for Yankee ironclads on the Cape Fear River.

Most times my street is peaceful. The houses have front porches with rocking chairs and wicker furniture and there are flowers blooming profusely in pots and around the steps. A tranquil, shady street that exudes peacefulness.

Like my neighbors, I too had a porch that overlooked the street. And my porch was where the firemen had gathered. I ran the rest of the way to my steps and mounted them in a rush, shouting, "What's wrong? What's happened?"

A pall of greasy smoke hung in the air. "This is my house," I told the firemen. "Where's the fire?"

"Everything's under control, ma'am," one fireman told me. "Just a little kitchen fire."

"Kitchen fire!" I screamed.

A defiant Patsy stood in the doorway. "If'n you had a decent cast iron skillet like every other good Southern woman, this wouldn't have happened. But no, y'all got them fancy Cuisinart pans. And they can't take the heat. I was heatin' up lard for my fried chicken and just popped into the parlor for a quick peek at Jimmy's latest find when the dang pan started burnin'."

The fireman who had helped rescue Jon and who had attended Binkie's book signing chimed in, "Good thing you've got smoke detectors all over the house because they went off and your neighbor called in the fire."

A fire in the kitchen! Smoke all through the house! And what was that about a "find" in the parlor?

I pushed past Patsy to see the damage. If my hands could

have fit around her neck, I would have wrung it.

The first thing I saw through the drifting greasy smoke was that my authentically restored parlor was cluttered with junk. I have decorated my house meticulously with inherited antiques, fine selections from the Castle Street antique district, and with choice items from The Ivy Cottage. My sweet little Victorian ladies' chairs and swooning sofa were almost obliterated, piled high with junk: picture frames without pictures or with cracked glass, chipped vases and crockery, and items I couldn't even identify.

The middle of the room was heaped with furniture: a table missing a leg laying on its side, a corner cabinet with broken doors, and a console table with a hole where the drawer should have been. All of it incredibly dirty, and no drop cloth spread under the junk to protect my oriental rugs.

My hands balled up into fists and I started to shake. Filled with mounting rage, I made my way into the kitchen. My camel and green antique gas stove that I'd had refitted so I could cook on it was black with soot. My Cuisinart frying pan was nowhere to be seen, but the kitchen sink was stopped up, filled with greasy water, and the cabinet above the sink was charred.

"Never try to put out a grease fire by pouring water on it," the fireman behind me said. "Just makes it worse. The fire flamed up and scorched your cabinet. We carried the flaming pan outside and poured sand in it."

I gave him a look like he was crazy. I hadn't done this. Why was he lecturing me? I had bought the pans because I was hoping to prepare meals for Jon and me. But now, seeing this kitchen disaster, I reaffirmed my commitment to restaurants and take-out food. Both were solidly back in my life from this day forward. No home cooking for me.

I hurried past the fireman and out into the hall, cursing her name. "Patsy! Patsy!" I was going to throw her out on her huge rump and her skinny-assed husband on his too. But Patsy was nowhere to be found. And their pickup truck that had been parked in front of my neighbor's house was gone as well.

The firemen were leaving. "Keep the doors and windows open and let this place air out," one advised.

Instantly my temper flared again and I was about to say something rash when I realized none of this was his fault. The firemen had just tried to help.

"Thank you for coming," I said. "I'll let it air out."

I sank down into the swing on my front porch and watched them drive away. I even managed a grateful wave. Then I got out my cell phone and dialed Melanie. This was all her fault.

"You've got to get that woman out of here," I screamed when Melanie answered the phone. "She practically burned down my house."

"Ashley, don't get your knickers in a knot. I just got off the phone with Patsy. She told me there had been a little accident and that you had over-reacted and I can hear in your voice that you have."

"Over-reacted? Melanie! She almost burned my house down! There is greasy smoke everywhere and my cabinets are scorched, my sink is ruined."

"Your sink? I thought the fire was in a skillet."

"Oh, forget it. Just get that woman out of here."

"You've got to stop carrying on like a drama queen, Ashley. You are being much too theatrical. Now listen, I was just about to call you. The Verandas had a cancellation for tomorrow so Patsy and Jimmy will be out of your house tomorrow afternoon."

"No, Melanie, today! Right away! Right now! I am going up to my room and I'm tossing all of their stuff down the stairs and out into the street. That is how much I despise those people."

"Oh, Ashley, you do make such a fuss over everything. I have nowhere to put them. It won't kill you to wait one more day."

"What is the hold up, Melanie? Why won't the police let them go back to Charlotte?"

"Oh some silly mix up over Jimmy's identity. He was a victim of identity theft last year and it still has not been sorted out. And with all the national attention to the stabbing in the bookstore, the police are being very, very careful. Dotting all the i's and crossing all the t's.

"Now listen, shug, just one more night and I'll owe you big time. Patsy says Jimmy will clean up your house like new. And she's having Cam and me over there tomorrow night for dinner so I'll check on everything myself. Plus, she says she's found the perfect house downtown and she is ready to make an offer."

"Oh right!" I said sarcastically. "She is delusional and so are you. She says she's buying Captain Pettigrew's house and for the last time, that house is not for sale!"

"Now don't go making decisions for your client, Ashley. I think Laura Gaston will come around when she hears the dollars Patsy is prepared to offer."

I groaned. She was a velvet steam roller. And could she be right? Might Laura Gaston sell it if the dollars were high enough? Might I find myself restoring the house for Patsy and Jimmy Pogue? If that were to happen, I think I would seriously contemplate throwing myself into the Cape Fear River — with a pair of cement Pradas on my feet!

"Look, shug, I've got another call I've got to take. I'll see you tomorrow night at your house. That Patsy is a fabulous cook. Her food will melt in your mouth. Bring Jon!"

And she was gone and I didn't even get a chance to tell her about how my parlor was being used as a warehouse for "pickins."

9

"I'd like to know," Patsy was saying to Cam Jordan, "why you are makin' a TV series from the books of an unknown mystery writer just because she writes about Wilmington when you could be makin' a series out of my books? Has nobody clued you in? I am the biggest mystery writer in North Carolina, and that other writer — well, heck, nobody never heard tell of her."

"Actually," Cam replied mildly, "I believe Kathy Reichs is the top-selling mystery writer in the state. But one of the cable networks beat me to her."

"Well then, you are lucky I am still available," Patsy crowed.

Melanie and I exchanged worried glances.

Patsy went on, "I've got name recognition. Instant name recognition, isn't that what sells in the entertainment industry?"

Poor Cam, he looked as brow beaten as Jimmy. Patsy had been haranguing Cam for at least an hour, ever since he arrived at my house. The fabulous dinner she had promised us was growing cold and dry in what used to be my kitchen, before it had been taken over by the Pogues.

Cameron Jordan was Melanie's fiancé. And she was fortunate to have him. After the bad boys she had been involved with, Cam Jordan was a regular prince of a guy. He was a very successful movie and television producer with his own studio here in Wilmington. And in the film business, Wilmington was the Hollywood of the East Coast.

Yet Cam was not at all egotistical or full of himself like many successful men. Instead, he came across as everyone's favorite big brother, modest but with a shy charm. Tall and lanky and maybe just a little bit clumsy, he had tousled sandy hair that he struggled to keep neat. He absolutely worshipped Melanie and treated her as if she had hung the moon.

He'd been giving her adoring looks ever since he arrived. We were all dressed in shorts, even Patsy which was a sight to behold, but Melanie always manages to look better than any other woman. She was stunning in simple white shorts and a green camisole. I had not had time to change, was still in my khakis and tee shirt, an outfit Melanie calls my "construction work chic."

Cam seemed to have recovered fully from Saturday's diving accident. Since Melanie hadn't mentioned it to me, I doubted he had told her yet — probably waiting for just the right moment. She had been tied up with her investors, and Cam was extremely busy with the filming of a pilot for the mystery series Patsy was knocking.

For the umpteenth time Cam patiently explained to Patsy, "Our market research studies demonstrate that TV viewers rate two topics as desirable for television viewing: that is, mysteries and old houses. When 'This Old House' aired a feature that was shot in Savannah about *Midnight in the Garden of Good and Evil*, that was a wake-up call for us in the business. That show drew a record viewing audience. So that's how I know a mystery series featuring old houses will go over big. My gut instinct tells me it will be a bigger success than my last series, 'Dolphin's Cove.' I had plenty of nay-sayers with that one as well and I proved them wrong."

Melanie tried to placate everyone for the mood was quickly becoming as heavy as the meal I'd caught a glimpse of in the kitchen. Melanie said, "Patsy, I can't wait to sample your delicious Southern cooking."

We were gathered on my patio in anticipation of Patsy's promised "dee-licious" dinner. Soft breezes played in the tree tops and birds twittered happily.

But Patsy was not twittering happily. And when Patsy was unhappy about something, nothing would do but that everyone around her had to be made miserable as well. She seemed to think that if she pounded a subject to death she would win the argument. Yet despite his easy going attitude and gentle manner, Cam was at his core a tough industry leader with a clear eye for what television viewers wanted to see. He was not about to be swayed by Patsy whom many saw as having already peaked and now was simply coasting along on past accomplishments.

"I've got the perfect set for this show right here in my own backyard. I don't have to send film crews around the state to other locations. Our historic district is the perfect setting. And the writing is bright and fresh. No stereotypes. Those novels about dysfunctional Southern families are last week's news. Dated and out of style. Let's face it, Patsy, the South has become a melting pot. I'm a perfect example. Came to Wilmington to produce a special for HBO, fell in love with the place, and relocated here."

His open arms sought to embrace the neighborhood. "Why, we've got Linda Lavin, Hilarie Burton, and Sydney Penny living within a few blocks of us. These old houses are being snapped up and restored by folks from all across the country, and Europe. Your kind of stories, about isolated, in-

bred, quirky Southern families are no longer in demand —
they're dated. Sorry, but those are the facts."

Patsy was quivering with hostility.

Still Cam sought to reason with her. "I imagine your publisher has told you that the small presses are cutting large
swaths into what used to be their exclusive markets. Alabaster
Publishing is a good example. It's local. They publish about a
dozen writers. Their premiere writer is founder Dixie Land . . ."
He snorted and held up his hand. "I know, I know, what a
name. But it's her real name and a PR person's dream. The
characters in her books reflect the way North Carolinians live
today; they're professionals with fine homes and kids in college,
with beach houses, and full and complicated lives.

"A lot of people are saying your characters are caricatures
that portray Southerners as uneducated and backward. Still, I'd
like to play fair with you. I'll be glad to have one of my assis-
tants take a second look at your books."

Patsy's face contorted with rage. She jumped up. "Don't go
doin' me no favors. I got where I am without a favor from
nobody. Now, I plum lost my appetite. And I sure as heck ain't
got no appetite for breakin' bread with you folks. Fact is, I never
want to lay eyes on any of your kind again."

She whirled on Melanie, who was hugging herself as if
bracing for the verbal pistol whipping she sensed was coming.

"You done lied to me from day one, missy. You led me to
believe Captain Pettigrew's house was for sale, but all I ever
heard out of Ashley's mouth was that it was not for sale."

Then she turned on me. "And you, little miss, you are the
worst kind of hostess. Whoever taught you your manners was
sadly delinquent. You know nothin' 'bout makin' a guest feel at
home. You go creepin' out of your own house without a word of
goodbye or leavin' us keys, like me and Jimmy were infected
with the bubonic plague. You got no food in your kitchen for
the hungry in your midst. And you make a fuss 'bout the least
littlest thing."

The doorbell was ringing at the front of the house but no one was brave enough to get up to answer the door. We were all taken aback by the intensity and suddenness of her attack, and were temporarily frozen in place.

I glanced at Jon and read controlled anger in his body language. And Cam looked guilty, as if he was somehow responsible for this outburst because he had refused to agree to give her the TV series she coveted.

"Come on, Jimmy," Patsy hollered. "We are out of here. I know when we ain't welcome and we ain't welcome here and never were." She moved toward the kitchen door that was standing open, a nonplused Jimmy in tow. He appeared almost bored. He had lived through these tirades too many times.

But Patsy wasn't finished. Before stepping through the kitchen door, she turned to deliver another tongue lashing. The doorbell shrilled again, silencing her momentarily, and Jon jumped up. "I'll get that." He squeezed by Patsy and hurried into the house.

I looked at Melanie and she looked at me. She was embarrassed. So was I. Poor Cam.

"We ain't got no choice but to spend the night here," Patsy declared. "Ain't got nowhere else to sleep. But first thing in the morning, we are outta here."

She turned back toward the house, but was blocked by Jon and the man he was leading out onto the patio.

Melanie jumped up and rushed forward. "Drew! I lost all track of time." She circled past Patsy and Jimmy, and grabbed the man by the hand. "Come on out and meet everybody. You've already met Jon. And this is his bride-to-be, my sister Ashley. And that's my fiancé Cam."

Melanie pointed us out, and Cam stood up, hand extended. I think we were all relieved for a break in the extreme tension.

The new arrival looked at us and smiled. If the scene seemed strained, or the introductions seemed rushed and awkward, he didn't reveal that he had noticed. Instead he asked, "Am I early? I thought you said eight, but I may have misunderstood."

"Oh, no, Drew, you are right on time." She turned him toward us. "Everyone this is Drew Ramsey. Drew leads a twelve-piece orchestra with three back-up singers. His group is called 'The Platinum Band' because they specialize in wedding parties. They are going to play for us, at our wedding reception."

"Oh," I exclaimed happily, and perked up. The wedding! I was instantly grateful. In the midst of her busiest weekend, Melanie had made time to continue planning our wedding. And Drew and his group would entertain. Now we were onto something positive. Patsy the "pain" would be out of my life tomorrow and things would get back to normal. We could resume the planning of the wedding, the restoration work on Captain Pettigrew's house, and partake of all the good things life had in store for us.

Drew was tall and fair, about Cam's size, but with the lean taut body of a runner. He was relaxed and had a nice smile. "Happy to meet you, Ashley," he said, and shook my hand.

I had already dismissed Patsy from my mind, so I was surprised to hear her say, "Hey there, Ramsey. How's your Harley?"

To my astonishment Patsy had made a complete about face and was all smiles. To us she said, "Me and Jimmy done met Drew at the bikers' meet in Myrtle Beach. Jimmy done restored classic Harleys for us, and Drew here has got himself the purtiest bike you ever done seen."

"I do remember you," Drew said, and reached to shake hands with both Patsy and Jimmy. "How you been? I gave up biking a while back. I run now and I've been meaning to take up diving."

Jon said, "Cam and I dive often. We'll take you out some-time with us. But you'll have to take lessons before you can go down."

Drew lit up. "Well hey, Jon, that's real nice of you and I'll be sure to take you up on the offer."

Patsy, her energy level restored, turned to Jimmy and said, "Jimmy, what are you waitin' for, help me carry out the food I done prepared. These folks are famished. We promised them a dinner they'd never forget and that is what they are gonna get."

I followed Patsy and Jimmy into the room I used to think of as *my* kitchen, before Patsy had taken over it, my house, and Lord a mercy, my life. Despite the open windows and doors and the ceiling fans stirring the breezes, the odor of singed grease hung in the air like gas fumes at a filling station. There were scorch marks on my cabinets and counter tops, and I reminded myself to get the insurance agent in here to assess the damage. If the sink had been scrubbed I couldn't tell because it was full of dirty plates and bowls.

Every pot and pan I owned had been put to use. I looked around at the mess and wanted to wring my hands. No, pull out my hair. No, pull out Patsy's long braid with one painful yank.

"We don't need no help in here, missy," Patsy said as if I had a nerve to barge into my own kitchen. "Me and Jimmy got things covered."

I pushed past Jimmy and reached for a cupboard door. "I'm setting the table. We decided to eat outside. It's a nice evening. Now excuse me while I get the plates."

I reached for my prized collection, a stack of blue and white Spode dinner plates.

"No, no, no," Patsy said, coming up behind me and firm-ly closing the cupboard door on my hand. "Not those. Me and Jimmy just found us a set of Fiesta Ware at a little hidey-hole shop downtown and Jimmy's been scrubbin' those plates all afternoon. We're usin' them."

I rubbed my bruised and pulsating hand and glared at her. Then I had second thoughts. Did I really want my beautiful collection of plates exposed to the Pogues? Did I want Patsy or Jimmy handling them? No!

I reminded myself that she would be gone in less than twenty-four hours and heaved a huge sigh of relief. "OK. Suit yourself. But please put all of my things back where you found them when you're finished in here."

"Ooooh. Touchy, touchy," and she mimicked my voice.

In a huff I fled the kitchen.

10

"That woman!" I cried to Jon and joined him on a chaise where he snuggled me. "She sure knows how to get to me."

"She'll be gone tomorrow," he reminded me. "Stay over at my house tonight. We'll go straight to work tomorrow morning. Then in the afternoon you can come back here and reclaim your house again."

"Oh, yes, please Lord," I sighed.

Melanie and Drew Ramsey were discussing musical selections. "We'll play the traditional songs like . . ."

"Not 'Daddy's Little Girl'," Melanie interrupted. "Our father is deceased. Skip that one. It'll just make us cry. And this is a joyful occasion."

"You don't know how joyful," Cam said.

"I've got two requests," I said. "Please sing, 'At Last.' That is Jon's and my favorite song. And I've always thought Anne Murray's 'Could I Have This Dance for the Rest of My Life' is especially romantic."

"Good choices, Ashley," Drew said. "We play a lot of the classics. All those old fox trots that Rod Stewart made popular again. Then we spice up the mix with something bouncy like 'Betty Lou' and you'll see, your guests will be out on the dance floor. I've brought a demo for you to listen to and I'll fax a list of our most popular songs so you can go over that."

"As long as I get to dance with my gorgeous wife, you can play music from Sesame Street," Cam said with a laugh, reminding us of how much his marriage to Melanie meant to him. How long he had waited for her to come around.

"Tell us something about yourself, Drew," Jon asked.

"Glad to. I'll fax you my resume if you want. My background is in classical music. I studied piano at Juilliard for a while, then with private instructors. On weekends we'd do gigs at weddings and parties and I got so I really liked that . . ."

Patsy came bustling out with two huge platters. "Wait till y'all taste my fried chicken," she said in a loud voice, cutting off our conversation. "Oh yum, I make it just like my mama used to. Y'all are gonna love it. And we've got mashed potatoes with lots of butter, and fried okra."

By now it was dark with only hurricane lanterns and ambient city light to illuminate the table. But we were hungry.

Jon helped himself to a drumstick. "There is only one way to eat fried chicken," he said, "and that is with your fingers."

"You are my kinda man," Patsy said jovially. What was happening? Where had all the fury gone? With a large serving fork she lifted a breast off the platter and plunked it onto Drew's plate. "You're the guest. And I know how to treat my guests." And she flicked a contemptuous glare my way. "The best for the guest." Then she laughed heartily. "So tell me, Drew, how long you been livin' in Wilmington?"

Drew struggled to cut the breast meat into pieces, but that was impossible. Finally, like the rest of us, he picked up the large piece of chicken and bit into it. "Oh my, this is good."

"It is, Patsy," I seconded, so glad that her histrionics were over. Maybe I could survive the evening and tomorrow she'd be gone. The first two bites of my wing were heavenly. But with the third bite I tasted too much fat and too much salt.

I set the wing on my plate, hoping Patsy would not notice that I wasn't eating.

But old eagle-eye said, "What's the matter with your appetite, young'un? Don't you like my cookin'?"

"Oh, no, Patsy, it's not that. It's just that I've been using olive oil for about a year now so I've lost my taste for butter. I mean, butter tastes so rich to me now."

"That ain't butter," Patsy declared. "I soak my chicken in buttermilk and fry it in Crisco shortening, same way my mama did. And don't go givin' me no lectures 'bout cholesterol. Everythin' my mama ate came out of a fryin' pan, fried in the drippins she done saved in a can. And Mama lived to be a hundred and one. I aim to, too."

"I'm sure you will," I said feebly.

Oh, please God, let this evening end, I prayed. And finally it did, after Patsy served dessert, bread pudding that she told us she made with Krispy Kreme glazed donuts instead of bread! I'd never sleep a wink that night. The sugar and fat surge was bouncing around in my arteries like radioactive ping pong balls.

After Cam and Melanie left with Drew Ramsey, and Patsy and Jimmy had stacked the dishes on the drain board, promising to wash up in the morning, Jon and I sat for a while in my front porch swing and watched the lights go out up and down Nun Street. We held hands and it was nice not to talk, to just sit quietly and love each other. We heard when Patsy and Jimmy stomped up the stairs to "their" room.

"Jon, you're right with your plan for how we will live after we are married. We'll live here in my house during the work week, then spend weekends at your house at Wrightsville

Beach. I can't wait until the Pogues leave so we can get our life back."

In answer, he squeezed my hand. "Life is good," he said.

"I've got to get some clean clothes for tomorrow," I told him. "I've worn every outfit I had at your house. I'll just go up quietly. According to Patsy, 'Jimmy done moved my things into the guest room,' so I won't have to disturb them, just grab some shorts and a couple of tee shirts. I'll be right back."

I climbed the stairs quietly, then turned at the newel post and made my way toward the front of the house where the master bedroom was located. The guest room came first, its door closed.

A soft light shone from the master bedroom and the door stood open. Patsy and Jimmy must have thought that we had left and that they were alone. Well, I'd be as quiet as a mouse and be gone in a second. Softly I started to open the door to the guest room. I'd be in and out before Patsy and Jimmy knew I was there. Then, I asked myself resentfully: This is *my* house, why am I tiptoeing around?

Because your mama and I raised you to be considerate of others, my daddy's voice whispered in my ear.

And then I heard something that stopped me cold. Jimmy's voice. Jimmy was speaking. "Cam Jordan told you what I've been telling you all along. I told you — no, I begged you — to start another series. Something relevant to the times. But no, you wouldn't listen. Now your publisher has passed on your latest manuscript. And where is the money going to come from?"

Patsy's tone was sarcastic, "Funny you should ask. Why don't you get yourself a profession for a change instead of treating me like the cash cow?"

Jimmy's tone was bitter. "Excellent choice of words. You know very well why I have no profession of my own. I have spent a lifetime helping you. I've devoted my life to making a success of yours. And now, the only thing I ever wanted — that house — and I can't have it because there's no money coming in except for some paltry royalty checks. I told you and I told you to make an offer on that house when Laura Gaston was still in medical school, when she was broke. She would have gone for it. We could have snapped it up for a song. But no, you never listen. You always know best."

"And how many times did I tell you to strike a match to that house when it was empty and no one was interested in restoring it?" Patsy countered.

Strike a match? What was that about? But I was embarrassed with my eavesdropping. I turned and tiptoed away, down the hall, skirting the squeaky floor board to hurry down the stairs. I'd wear dirty clothes tomorrow.

At the foot of the steps enlightenment caused me to stop abruptly. Jimmy could not only speak, but he could speak very well. The voice I'd heard was cultivated and educated. And so was Patsy's! That illiterate country whine she put on was a fake!

And the Pogues, whom Melanie thought were loaded, were in reality broke.

I stepped quietly out onto the porch, eager to tell Jon what I'd just heard. Across the street, my neighbor was wheeling his trash barrel out to the curb. "Oh shoot, I completely forgot," I told Jon. "Tomorrow morning is trash pick-up. Help me take the trash can and the recyclable bin down to the curb."

"Sure," he replied, and started down the porch steps. We skirted around the porch and under the porte cochere to the side rear corner of the house where the garbage containers were stored.

"Wow, they've been busy," I said.

My trash barrel was filled to the brim, so full that the lid did not fit closely. I wheeled the barrel while Jon lifted and carried the recyclable bin which was loaded with bottles.

As I parked the trash barrel on the curb, I noticed a bit of bright white plastic sticking out from under the lid. "What's this?" I asked Jon. "Didn't Binkie say . . .?" And I pulled the white padded vinyl envelope from the trash can.

"What . . .?" Jon started to ask. "Oh . . ."

I carried it over to the street lamp. "It's a FedEx envelope. And it's addressed to Binkie." I pulled open the flap. Empty.

"How did Binkie's stolen envelope get into my trash barrel?"

11

On Tuesday morning Jon and I picked up Binkie and drove to Two Sisters Bookery. On the way we discussed our latest discoveries. "They're broke," I told Binkie. "And they deposited your envelope in my trash barrel." I handed him the envelope.

"Should we turn it over to the police?" Binkie asked.

"I wonder what we should do with it too," Jon said.

I said, "I know that Patsy did not steal your briefcase. She was not at Two Sisters on Saturday. She is not someone you overlook. I'd have seen her."

"But Jimmy is someone you overlook easily," Jon said.

"Yes, Jimmy does tend to blend into the background," Binkie agreed.

"By this time, there will be so many fingerprints on that envelope, it will be useless as evidence," I speculated.

"I quite agree, Ashley dear," Binkie said. "FedEx employees have handled that envelope, as have I. Perhaps the dead man, Hugh Mullins, his killer, Patsy and Jimmy Pogue, you, Jon."

"And since it was found at my house and has my fingerprints on it — well, Diane Sherwood will have a field day."

"I suspect the envelope will reveal only smudges at this point. I say we should hold onto it for a while. See where the police's investigation leads them," Binkie said. "Not that I condone withholding evidence from the police, but in this case, let's just sit on the envelope for a day or two. After all, Ashley, if you had not spotted it, it would be on a trash truck right now."

Jon and I could not argue with his reasoning. We'd wait.

At Two Sisters the crime scene tape had been removed, and Cathy Stanley was once again presiding over a popular bookstore.

"Curiosity seekers," Cathy confided.

"We don't want to disturb you," I told her. "We just want to have a look around. You understand."

"Go ahead, join the crowd," she replied. "I felt the same way. I had to see for myself that the body was gone. Look all you want. My bookstore has become a sight-seeing attraction." She managed a smile. Plucky lady.

We three moved to the rear of the bookstore, to the far corner where Binkie's book signing had taken place. "There it is," Binkie declared, and he scooped up the leather-bound journal from the crowded book shelf where he had left it.

"Now how are we going to get it out of here?" I asked.

"Not to worry," Binkie said. "Cathy would never question me. I will simply carry it out openly in my hand as if it belongs to me. And, indeed, it does. There are some advantages to age, and one of them is that people do not suspect you of stealing."

"I need to take a peek at the storage room," I said. "I know it's macabre, but Cathy is right, I need to reassure myself the body is no longer there."

"Oh, Ashley, don't look. Please, just try to forget that grisly sight," Jon said worriedly.

"I've got to look," I replied, and pushed open the screen door. Nothing. Just the same shelves and file cabinets, the mini-refrigerator, the tiny desk. No body lay curled on the black and white tile floor. No stolen briefcase. No knife. But as I looked closer in the florescent light, one thing remained: blood. The rusty stain on the floor was blood.

At the front door, a family of five was leaving just as we were, and we walked out with them, giving Cathy a friendly goodbye. She did not see the journal Binkie carried.

Jon drove us to Binkie's house. When we were settled in the study with Aunt Ruby and tall glasses of iced tea, Binkie opened the journal and quickly turned the pages, giving each a cursory examination.

"Another letter," he said, withdrawing a document.

"Read it to us," I invited.

"And so I shall. It is dated November 4, 1862, and it's addressed to Mrs. Pettigrew.

Dearest Mother,

I am entrusting this letter to the esteemed Captain Maffitt with faith that he will present it and himself to you in the near future. Mother, news of the severity of the Yellow Fever epidemic at home has reached me here in Nassau. I implore you to take my little sister Lacey and your most cherished self and flee to Aunt Martha in Robeson County. My good aunt will take you in despite rumors I have heard that our townsfolk are being turned away from distant counties which through God's mercy have been spared this deadly scourge. Mother, if you will commence with the burning of rosin in barrels along our property on Front Street, Captain Maffitt assures me you will ward off the disease.

I have a second motive for urging you to withdraw from Wilmington for the season, for I have heard from first-hand witnesses how the streets of our genteel city have turned mean with the presence of coarse British sailors and the establishment of bawdy houses in our port. I fear for your safety and for Lacey's inno-cence.

I know, Mother, that you are dedicated to assisting Mrs. Martin and Mrs. deRossett with the work of the Soldiers' Aid Society. I admire you and those good ladies for your sacrifices and I know our brave Confederate lads are grateful for the clothing and blankets you sew for them and for the nourishing home-cooked meals you serve them as they pass through our railroad depot. Even so, I implore you to quit Wilmington as soon as you and Lacey are able to pack your bags and secure the house. You will be safe with Aunt Martha and I shall not have the worry of my darlings to bur-den me as I ply the Atlantic.

Here is an account of what has befallen your son since we bade farewell on the dock of our own Cape Fear River. The Mariner steamed down river without incident. We took cover along the shoreline until darkness fell. Under the pitch black of a moonless sky, I piloted us safely across the bar at New Inlet. Scarcely had we rounded Ft. Fisher than we were spotted by a Federal man-of-war. That blockader gave chase and fired upon us. The Captain gave the order to increase the steam but before we could outrun our pursuer, missiles from the warship hit their mark, resulting in damage to the wheelhouse

From the fort, Colonel Lamb witnessed our distress and com-menced firing the Whitworth rifle guns at the Union ships. Under the protection of Ft. Fisher's mighty guns, we were able to elude the blockader, making a dash through the outer blockade for Nassau which we reached safely despite the damage.

After off-loading our cargo of cotton and tobacco into the warehouses, we put in for repairs to the wheelhouse. I am forced to remain here awaiting consignment to another crew.

I hope that when I return to Wilmington, Dear Mother, you and Lacey will be safely ensconced with Aunt Martha, far from the threat of Yellow Jack. I will be sad not to see you, but my heart will be full of gratitude knowing that you are safe. I know that we will be together again when the azaleas bloom. You are in my prayers each night. I will keep you apprised of my whereabouts through letters which I shall dispatch with only the most trustworthy of seamen. Please send word through Captain Maffitt that you are leaving for Aunt Martha's home and I will direct future missives to you in Robeson County.

I remain your loving and devoted son,

Thomas Pettigrew.

P.S. All of my love to little Lacey. Tell her I shall write to her soon. TP

"Binkie, is Captain Pettigrew's description of Wilmington during the blockade accurate? Was it a mean place?"

"Oh my, yes, Ashley. Most of the blockade runners were not a part of the Confederate navy, you know, therefore not under strict military supervision. Many sailors were merchants and profiteers. And they were paid in gold, while the Confederate soldiers were paid half in gold and half in Confederate currency. A river pilot like Captain Pettigrew could earn as much as $3000 for one successful trip up the Cape Fear. It was a time of inflation."

"That means there was a lot of money flowing through the town," I said.

"That is true, Ashley, but it rarely benefited our townsfolk. They suffered dearly from shortages of basic necessities during the war. And the privateer sailors spent their earnings on drink and brothels, so the city became quite coarse, I am afraid."

"Daddy always said slavery was a great evil. One man should never own another. Still, the Civil War was such a tragedy — brother fighting brother. And my heart goes out to the innocent victims of the war, to Mrs. Pettigrew and little Lacey, whose lives were thrown upsidedown. And to the

Captain too, forced to leave home for long periods of time, and to risk his life on the sea."

"True, Ashley," Binkie agreed. "If the Union navy could have sailed up the Cape Fear they would have taken Wilmington, which eventually did happen, so men like Captain Pettigrew were fighting to save their homes from invasion."

Binkie nodded sadly. "As you say, a tragedy for our nation."

12

Work was progressing nicely on the Captain's house. Paint crews had arrived and had begun applying a white base coat to the restored exterior walls. At the same time, carpenters continued to replace the siding on the south wall and then they would be finished.

Inside, I made a mental note to myself to clean the fireplace surround tiles just as soon as the dusty phase of the restoration was behind us. I took a late lunch break, left my van at the site, and walked home to check on my house.

I enjoy long walks around the historic district which provides an opportunity to admire other restorations in progress. So many old houses are getting a second change. And on empty lots, infill houses were being built in the style of the district. The historic district was experiencing revitalization.

Nun Street was quiet in the early afternoon. The day was heating up but a pleasant breeze rustled through the treetops and small white clouds scudded across the sky. Sultry weather had not yet struck. Approaching The Verandas B&B, I saw Jimmy Pogue heft two large black duffel bags into the back of his white pickup truck, then climb into the cab. He pulled away from the curb in a great rush, wheels spinning. I did not have a view of the passenger side of the truck but assumed Patsy was in there with him.

So they were actually leaving! Nothing could make me happier, although I did wonder why they were not checking into The Verandas. Oh, what did I care, I thought, as long as they were out of my house. Perhaps, they could not afford the elegant Verandas unless someone else like my sister was footing the bill. Jimmy had not seen me and for that I was grateful. I certainly did not want another confrontation with the Pogues. I'd had enough. Good riddance, was what I was thinking.

I'd just check on my house and if there were issues that needed to be resolved, well, I'd take them up with Melanie. More than anything I wanted their junk-furniture out of my parlor. I confess to being particular about my surroundings. I'd grown up in a lovely home on Summer Rest Road and Mama and Daddy had furnished it nicely. Mama had been a wonderful decorator, and made every room look pretty. I guess I had inherited my decorating talent from her. Mama would have been as horrified as I at Patsy's collecting junk off the street and bringing it into her home.

I still could not get over my discovery that the Pogues were capable of speaking perfectly good English. Why ever did Patsy put on that terrible redneck accent? It just didn't make any sense. I could understand why Jimmy rarely spoke; he rarely got the chance. Patsy was larger than life, an overwhelming force. Still, Jimmy had stood up to her last night. In fact, I'd registered a great deal of hostility and resentment in his voice. He'd devoted his life to her career, and apparently that was now floundering and he blamed her failure on her unwillingness to take advice from him. She was head-strong and pig-headed.

Jon had been as mystified as I when I'd told him what I'd overheard on our drive to his house last night. At ten o'clock

100

we'd reached the ICW just as the drawbridge was being raised to allow a parade of tall ships to pass through.

Jon had cut the engine and we'd taken a moment to walk to the railing to watch the ships float gracefully by. What is it about a summer night that makes the air feel like silk against your skin? Jon slipped his arm around my waist and we leaned in close to each other. We stood there and watched the beautiful spectacle unfold. A bright moon drifted in and out of the clouds. On Harbour Island the Blue Water Restaurant was lit up like a Mississippi Showboat.

I like it that while Jon and I never run out of words, our silences are just as meaningful. We communicate even when not speaking: the silent communication of lovers. I rested my head on his shoulder and he pressed his cheek to the top of my head. We stood that way for a long moment, rejoicing in our togetherness. Then the bridge ramps began their descent and we hurried to the Escalade and jumped inside just as the line of traffic started to move.

On Nun Street, the front door at my house was standing open for all the world to enter. Just inside the reception hall, two suitcases waited. Why hadn't Jimmy taken these as well? And then I had a horrible thought: they hadn't left at all. I called Patsy's name but got no answer. Mounting the stairs, I called again. The guest room and the third bedroom were empty.

My own bedroom was a mess, looking like it had been ransacked. The bed was unmade but that was OK because I wanted to launder the sheets anyway. But Patsy's clothes had been dumped on top of the rumbled sheets, and a suitcase lay open at the foot of the bed. And then to my dismay I saw that she had scattered face powder across the top of my great-grandmother's rosewood dressing table. I almost cried. I cherished my family heirlooms. Face powder would be difficult to remove from the old wood without rubbing it into the grain. Darn that Patsy! Who wore face powder in this day and age? No wonder her face always looked pale and pasty.

In the bathroom — my house has only one and it is old-fashioned with a stained glass window, white tile, and a tub that sits up on clawed feet — I found long gray hairs in the pedestal sink. Oh, yuck! Something told me I'd be finding evidence of Patsy Pogue's presence long after she was gone.

Back downstairs, the parlor was still cluttered with the broken, grimy furniture they'd culled from curbside cast-offs. "Patsy!" I yelled, determined to have it out with her. She had to get out, completely, lock, stock and barrel. Barrel? Who could tell? There might have actually been a barrel hidden under all that junk. Even in my distraught state, I managed to chuckle at that image.

In the kitchen I discovered that Patsy had been cooking again. Another dessert! As if the bread pudding she had made from glazed donuts had not been enough to satisfy anyone's sweet tooth for a month. A pan of fudge brownies topped with what looked like brown sugar and pecans sat on the counter. There was an open tub of gooey caramel. And a plate of chopped nuts had traces of ice cream in it. The carton of vanilla ice cream beside the plate was melting. Automatically, I picked up the carton, replaced the lid, and shoved it into the freezer.

Two servings of brownie had been removed from the pan. And a spoon coated with hardening caramel was stuck to the countertop. Nut crumbs were scattered everywhere. The dishes from last night's dinner had not been washed as promised, merely shifted into the second sink bowl.

Even with the kitchen door standing wide open, the smell of scorched wood from Monday's fire hung in the air. I stepped off my kitchen porch to search for Patsy in the backyard.

My azalea bushes had grown large and had flowered magnificently during the spring; now they were thick with green leaves. There was a huge magnolia tree at the far edge of my garden and it was in full, sweet bloom. But no Patsy.

How could she and Jimmy leave without closing and locking the doors? Were they that irresponsible?

My charming Victorian gazebo stood in the center of the garden with narrow walkways leading to it from the four corners of the yard. It was covered with Carolina jessamine that bloomed almost all year round. A flash of memory of Nick took me by surprise. Two years ago, before we had married, when he had been a homicide detective with Wilmington PD, he and Diane Sherwood had arrived at my house during an Azalea Festival tour in progress. They had come to question me about the death of a former Azalea Belle, and I'd led them out here to the gazebo where we could talk in private. I had sensed that Diane was smitten with Nick. But when we sat in the gazebo and Nick selected a seat at a distance from Diane, I knew he did not share her feelings.

So now Nick was back in Wilmington. It would be impossible for me not to bump into him. Wilmington might have a population of a hundred thousand, yet it is a small town in many ways, especially the historic district. I wondered what I would feel when I saw him. It had been seven months since we parted. Two years ago, when we had married, I had been madly in love with him. They say love is blind. For me that had been true. I had worn blinders that prevented me from seeing that Nick had a wanderlust and a thirst for adventure that would make it impossible for him to find satisfaction in domestic life.

And domestic life was exactly what I was committed to — I loved decorating, turning a house into a home, and entertaining my loved ones in that home. The people I loved — Jon, Melanie, Aunt Ruby, and Binkie — had always held

Nick apart, treating him with respect but with a reserve that was not natural to them.

Last November had been a low point in my life. I was still mourning the loss of the baby that I'd miscarried early in my pregnancy. Then I'd discovered that Nick was having an affair with a canine handler whom he'd met at Blackwater Security. Now, it seemed, he had grown disillusioned with that outfit as well. I wondered if the Captain would take him back into the police department.

Jon's steady love had lifted me out of my depression and had given me the power to recover. I had always loved him as my best friend, now I loved him as my future husband.

I gave myself a hug. You are one lucky girl, Ashley Wilkes, I told myself. I wandered to the gazebo to sit for a moment before tackling the mess inside the house.

And that's where I found Patsy Pogue. She was lying on the brick floor, curled on her side. The dinner plate had fallen from her hand and broken. Had she experienced a stroke? With the way she gorged on fats and sugar, a stroke seemed inevitable.

Shards of glass from one of my lovely blue and white Spode plates pierced the mounds of whipped cream, ice cream, fudge brownies, and scoops of hardening caramel.

Patsy was wearing a red tent-like shirt. At her middle, a huge darker red stain had soaked through the cotton. I experienced déjà vu. Patsy had been killed exactly like the man I'd stumbled upon at Two Sisters. She had been stabbed. A knife handle protruded from her abdomen in precisely the same way. It is weird what runs through one's mind at such a time, but I wondered if the knife had come from my set of chef's knives and I hoped not. Although that would make no difference.

For as Patsy had stood in my gazebo, feasting on a wicked dessert of fudge brownies with every conceivable topping, someone had crept up behind her, reached around her waist, and thrust a knife up and under her sternum.

I didn't scream. I could scarcely breathe. I pulled my cell phone from my waist band, about to call 911, when the phone chirped.

"Ashley, it's me," Melanie said.

"Melanie, I can't talk now," I cried.

"I can't either. I'm showing a house. But I just wanted to let you know that I'm sending a cleaning crew over to your house to clean up after Patsy and Jimmy."

"No!" I screamed.

"Now, shug, it's the least I can do for you after you put up with the Pogues."

"Melanie, shut up! Patsy is dead. She's been murdered."

"What!"

"Just like that man at Two Sisters. She's been stabbed."

"Call the cops. I'm coming right over."

13

Just as Cathy Stanley had been driven out of her book-shop, I was being driven out of my house by a squadron of homicide detectives and a CSI team. And with the squalor in my house, processing it was going to take a while, Detective Diane Sherwood was delighted to tell me.

She cast a disapproving eye upon the mess in my kitchen. Surely she didn't think I . . . "Patsy was cooking before she . . ." I didn't finish the sentence. Who cared if the kitchen was a mess? Why did this woman get on my last nerve? There was a dead body in my gazebo, for pity sakes!

Again and again I repeated my story. How I'd come home to find the front and back doors standing open, how I'd searched the house for Patsy, then found her body in the gaze-bo. This time when the CSI teck ran the lumalite over me, it did not detect a speck of blood. I had not knelt beside Patsy. She was dead and I had learned a lesson.

"What was your relationship with the dead woman?" Diane wanted to know.

"I didn't have a relationship with her," I replied, exasper-ated. "I was letting her stay here as a favor to Melanie. She is one of Melanie's investors. Why are you questioning me? I didn't kill her!

"Listen, Diane, you should be searching for her husband Jimmy. He took off right before I found Patsy. You should put out one of those All Points Bulletins or whatever you call them."

"Why? Do you have a reason for thinking that Jimmy Pogue killed his wife?" she asked in a disbelieving and infuriating tone.

I tilted my head from side to side like a confused puppy. She was in law enforcement; weren't they trained to suspect the spouse first? Meanwhile, Jimmy Pogue was hightailing it to parts unknown.

It was maddening how cool this woman could remain in the most heated circumstances. I was forced to repeat the quarrel I had overheard last night.

"Don't answer any more questions, Ashley!" Melanie shouted as she pushed past the uniformed officer who was attempting to block her way. Melanie turned on him, furious. "Take your hands off me! This is my sister's house. I can come in here whenever I want. My father was a judge — I know the law!"

Diane Sherwood crossed her arms over her chest and smirked. I knew exactly what she was thinking: The Wilkes sisters are as nutty as a Snickers bar.

Melanie took hold of my arm. "Get your purse. We are out of here." To Diane she said, "If you want to talk to either of us, call our lawyer, Walt Brice."

Walter Brice was the best defense attorney in New Hanover County and had been a friend of our late father, Judge Peter Wilkes.

Bolstered by Melanie's assertiveness, I said to Diane, "Make sure you lock up when you are through. If anything is missing, I'll hold you and the PD responsible."

Diane gave the junk stacked in my parlor a contemptuous once over. "As if you'd know if something was missing."

"Why does that woman hate me so much?" I asked Melanie after she had hustled me down my front steps and into her waiting Mercedes convertible which she'd left double parked in Nun Street. Police cars had filled all available curb spots. My own car was parked in the porte cochere at the side entrance to my house — the only entrance not standing wide open for all the world to see the mess inside my house — and I'd left my van at the Captain's house on Front Street.

"She hates you because she fears you," Melanie said.

"Fears me!" Why would anyone fear me?

Melanie took Third Street to Oleander and headed east. "Where are we going?" I asked, the wind catching and blowing my hair as Melanie accelerated.

"I know just what we need to take our minds off these dreadful killings." She turned to me. "They have nothing to do with us, you know. Here I am, just doing my job, organizing my investors and showing desirable properties, and it's like I spawned a coven of witches!"

"Watch where you're driving!" I screeched. If I had a dollar for every time I said that one, I'd be a millionaire.

"She fears you because she sees you as a rival and you're younger and prettier. I've had to put up with her type of female all of my life. I know how snotty they can act. She'll make your life miserable if you let her."

"But she's the police, Melanie, and I'm involved in two homicides. It's not my fault that I find the victims, but Diane Sherwood acts like I'm guilty of something just because I do. I'm innocent. If anyone's to blame, it's you for bringing that dreadful Patsy into my house!"

"Don't go there! You're playing into Sherwood's hands with that kind of attitude. She'd love to split us up — divide and conquer. But as long as we stick together — and as long as you stand up to her — we'll beat her at her game. And when she starts to put on the pressure, just call Walt Brice. He'll take care of her."

"This is all about Nick," I groaned. "She wanted Nick, and I got him and that is what makes her so spiteful. Hard to believe that I once respected her. Not anymore. I told her she was welcome to Nick, but that doesn't seem to make any difference."

"That's because Nick didn't want her then and I doubt he wants her now. She probably thinks he is still hung up on you. That's her problem, not yours. So let it go. You're lucky he's out of your life. I've been telling you that for months. Now forget all the homicide stuff. We've got a wedding to plan. We've got the best men in our lives, real catches. Diane and Nick are welcome to each other. Together they don't make enough money to pay my dry cleaning bill. You've got to learn to focus, Ashley, like I do. Don't let the enemy camp distract you."

I gave her a look of renewed respect. "You know something, big sis, you're something else. Sometimes it's uncanny how much you remind me of Daddy. That sounds just like something he'd say."

Melanie flashed a megawatt smile my way. The wind whipped her long auburn hair but it only fell perfectly back in place. "The apple doesn't fall far from the tree."

"In your case, I'd say it's a peach, big sis. OK, now where are we going?" I repeated.

"Why, to try on wedding dresses. What else? Nothing will make you feel more like a bride and get you back on target than a long white gown."

Wedding dresses. Yes, it was certainly time. "Thank goodness we're not living in Mama's era. Divorced women weren't allowed to wear wedding gowns when they remarried, and certainly not white gowns. The bride would have been ostracized."

"Well, thank goodness society has progressed. Oh, did I tell you? Candy Murray is meeting us. She publishes a Southern wedding magazine, you know. And she has excellent taste."

Here we go again with the women with excellent taste, I thought. Why did they always turn out to be unreliable and trouble? And why was Melanie always taken in by them? "I've got to call Jon," I said, and hit his number on my cell phone.

After our conversation, I told Melanie, "He already knows about Patsy's murder. The whole town knows. He's standing on the sidewalk out in front of my house like the entire population of Wilmington!"

"Did you tell him where we're going?"

"No. Just that I was with you. Where are we going?"

"A bridal boutique, of course."

"Oh, shug, that one is definitely you," Melanie squealed.

"It's fabulous," Candy Murray agreed.

I was modeling a Jessica McClintock wedding gown, simple white strapless with a mid-length train. "You can wear Great-Aunt Lillian's rubies with that dress," Melanie advised.

She turned to Candy. "Since it's going to be a Christmas wedding, I want to inject red into the color scheme as much as possible."

I studied myself in the full-length mirror. I felt like a princess. My dark brown hair had grown longer and now skimmed my shoulders. The pure whiteness of the dress brought out the pink in my skin. My gray eyes looked huge. I looked like a bride. I looked like a princess. I felt like a queen.

"I think I'll wear my hair up," I said and lifted my hair off my neck.

Neither Candy nor Melanie responded, instead Candy told Melanie, "Shug, I can't tell you how much I admire you for planning your own wedding. You are really something. Most brides aren't capable and have to hire a professional."

"I think this is the one," I said, and saw my skin flush with happiness.

Melanie giggled and confessed, "I'm just a control freak. I know I can do a better job than a wedding planner."

"Well, if you need any help, just call me. I've got the contacts."

"Oh, Candy, you are a love," Melanie said.

Seeing myself in the gown, the wedding felt real. In December I really was going to be divorced from Nick. In December I really was going to marry Jon. Life is sure funny, I thought to myself. Funny and good.

"I think simple white peau de soie pumps," Candy said, looking me over in an analytical way. "Don't you, Melanie?"

"I agree. We don't want peek-a-boo toes with that elegant dress."

"Well, I'm glad you've got that settled," I said. Peek-a-boo toes, indeed. Yet actually, I was feeling very, very happy and grateful to both of them. I'd pushed Patsy Pogue's murder to the perimeter of my consciousness.

"Now, it's your turn, Melanie," Candy said. "Try on this ivory gown."

"Oh, I've already ordered my gown from Vera Wang. I selected it when Cam and I were in New York last month."

Candy was impressed. "She's the best. She made my friend Mary Susan's dress and you . . ."

I tuned them out and told the sales associate that this was the dress for me, and to get the alterations lady. As the gown was fitted and pinned — it was an almost perfect fit, needing only a few minor adjustments — I couldn't help but think that I was standing here very much alive while Patsy was no doubt still lying in my gazebo with police photographers and a medical examiner hovering over her, not giving her any peace. She had been a dreadful woman — but nobody deserved to be murdered.

Despite the exquisite and expensive tending that Candy Murray lavished upon her appearance, there was nothing she could do about her odd shape. From the waist up she looked like a Modigliani drawing: high forehead and long narrow horsy face. Long narrow torso, long thin arms. But then your eye stopped in alarm at her short, short legs and you blinked and wondered if your eyes were playing tricks on you. The cropped pants she was wearing didn't help; they shortened the appearance of her legs, as if her legs, not the pants, had been cropped. Now Melanie, with her perfect figure, and even I, with my not-so-perfect figure, can get away with Capri pants, but a short-legged woman like Candy could not.

What she lacked in stature, she made up for with determination and a super confident ego. "Why not?" was her favorite expression. Ask her anything, and her response was always a hearty "why not!" As if she was game for anything. As if there was no hurdle so high her short legs could not surmount it.

And she was cold. Deep, deep down, she was cold. Despite her gregarious and friendly manner, she was a chilly woman. It showed in her eyes when she thought you weren't noticing. An icy glint. Instinctively I didn't like her. Didn't trust her.

We decided to go to the Bridge Tender Restaurant for a drink, and to call our "men folk" to meet us there for dinner. But first we had to make a quick stop at Melanie's so I could borrow something decent to wear.

"What am I going to do for clothes while the police shut me out of my house?" I moaned on the drive to Melanie's house on Sandpiper's Cove. We were alone on the drive, Candy having something to do and deciding to meet us at the Bridge Tender in an hour. "Everything I have at Jon's is dirty. I haven't had a moment for laundry."

"You'll borrow my clothes. I think I have some things you can fit into."

And she did. In her bedroom, she produced a stretchy pink tank top with a pink linen loose shirt. "Don't button it and it will fit," she told me. "These pants have a draw string waist so they'll be fine."

Spunky, Melanie's cat, was winding himself around my ankles so that I could not get my feet out of my shorts. "Spunky, I'm happy to see you too." I lifted him and set him on the bed where he proceeded to groom his glossy black coat. He has a white fur bib that makes him look like he is wearing a tuxedo. Recently someone had told me that certain cats were "closet groomers" — grooming themselves only when no one was around. Spunky was certainly not a closet groomer.

"I like food too much," I complained as I stepped out of what Melanie calls my construction-wear chic outfit and into her elegant thin linen sportswear.

"Well, I do too. We just have different metabolisms, is all," she said. Her head was in the closet and she was pulling out clothing items. "These should do you for a few days."

Then she seemed to really see me for she stopped, and quickly crossed the room to close the distance between us. She enfolded me in a warm embrace. "Listen, baby sister, I don't say this often enough, but I love you. If anything had happened to you today . . . If you had arrived while the murderer was still there . . . Why, I just couldn't live without you. You are the most important person in the world to me."

She moved back and I saw that tears had welled up in her beautiful green eyes, making them sparkle.

I hugged her tight. "And you are the most important person in the world to me too. Don't cry, Mel. I'm safe and so are you. I don't know what's going on anymore, but as you say, it has nothing to do with us."

Melanie stepped back, thinking hard. "The key to all this is that journal. I think we need to do some investigating of our own. That Diane Sherwood is a sorry excuse for a detective. After dinner, we're going over to Binkie's and see what he's learned from the journal. Hugh Mullins was killed over it."

"And there was an attempted break-in at Binkie's house," I added, "and what else could they have been after but the journal?"

I had a thought. "Do you suppose the murderer was searching my house for the journal and then Patsy caught him and so he killed her?" I shook my head negatively. "No, that doesn't work. Patsy was out in the gazebo gobbling down fudge brownies. He snuck up behind her. So, no, she was killed for another reason."

Melanie gave me a searching look.

I went on, "I hate to admit it but you are right. We can't rely on Diane Sherwood. She wouldn't even listen when I told her about Jimmy's quarrel with Patsy and how he'd fled the murder scene. She's much too blinded by her dislike for me to analyze this crime dispassionately."

Melanie looked thoughtful. "But what could have happened during the height of the Civil War that would provide a motive for someone to kill now? Listen, little sis, if anyone is going to solve this crime and get the cops out of our hair so we can go back to planning our wedding, it will have to be us."

"Agreed," I said firmly. "And Jon and Cam can help."

ELLEN ELIZABETH HUNTER

14

The deck at the Bridge Tender Restaurant faces east on Motts Channel. The sun was setting behind us, painting the water a lively pink. White yachts anchored at the marina reflected the fiery sunset as well, their swaths of glass mirroring the sun blindingly. Across the channel, Blue Water Restaurant was doing a brisk business on their palm-studded deck. A gorgeous evening, much too lush and vital to befit the ending of the day when murder had been committed.

Over Kiss Martinis for the girls — Vodka and Baileys with cinnamon and sugar on the rim, kind of like getting dessert and an alcoholic kick at the same time — and Surfer Martinis — vodka with rum — for the boys, we talked the murder to death: no pun intended.

"Did you know Patsy Pogue?" I asked Candy.

Candy did a causal flip of her perfectly manicured and bejeweled white hand. "Oh, everybody knew Patsy. I don't think there's a woman's club in this state that has not had her as a guest of honor at one time or another. And I've bumped into her at fund raisers, weddings, that type event."

I wanted to ask how the luncheon guests managed to understand anything she said but I have been raised not to speak ill of the dead. Besides, many people find that kind of Beverly Hillbillies speak colorful. Instead I asked, "What's the story on her husband? He rarely said a word."

I omitted a description of how I'd seen Jimmy Pogue jumping into his truck and taking off while Patsy lay dead in my gazebo. I had told the police; let them deal with it. I was also curious to know if they had found fingerprints on the knife handles.

Candy's husband Bo said, "Ah, Jimmy Pogue. Now that's an interesting story. At one time he wrote a scholarly book on the fall of Ft. Fisher. A prestigious accomplishment, but not many takers. So when Patsy won all those awards that year, Jimmy threw himself into building her career. I understand he writes the more factual and difficult sections of her books, although he never gets credit."

"Something like a king builder," Candy said, then laughed. "Or rather a queen builder."

"You must have known Jimmy pretty well," I said to Bo.

A pleasure craft motored slowly by, its gentle wake lapping the pilings. Bo leaned back comfortably in his white vinyl chair.

"I knew him at Chapel Hill. He was an older student, a Vietnam vet. We graduated the same year. Both history majors. He was the scholar though, said he was going to teach one day. Which means a Ph.D. I don't think he ever got one. I took history because I like it. I always knew I'd take over my daddy's car dealership so I wasn't preparing for a career."

"I just don't understand who would want to kill Patsy," Candy said.

I wanted to say everyone who knew her, but kept my mouth shut.

Cam looked like he might repeat the disagreeable conversation he'd had with her when she had tried to persuade him to develop her books into a TV series, but must have thought better of it for he kept silent as well.

Melanie said, "Well, she sure fooled me. I thought she had money but Ashley overheard Patsy and Jimmy talking and he said they were out of money and that her editor had passed on her last manuscript. Yet she kept telling me she had the money to buy a large house downtown. Otherwise, I would have never included the Pogues in my investors week-end."

"Enough of this talk of murder," I said. "I'm hungry and I don't want my dinner spoiled with talk of Patsy. She was hard enough to take in life."

Unkind of me? Perhaps. But I was tired and hungry and therefore cranky.

"Yes, let's order," Melanie said. "This murder has nothing to do with us. It was a family matter."

"Family?" Bo asked. "You mean you think Jimmy killed Patsy? Some of those veterans do have problems."

"Enough," Jon said with finality. "Ashley's been through a lot lately. Too much for anyone to handle. But she's coping. Aren't you, sugar?" he asked, and lifted my hand off the table to kiss it.

This man was to die for! His reaction when he first saw me had been similar to Melanie's earlier expression of love. He'd grabbed me and pulled me to him fiercely and growled how grateful he was that I had not entered the house while the murderer was there.

I gave him an adoring look but took my hand back and used it to open the menu. Ummm, everything sounded so good! "Oh, look! Prosciutto Wrapped Salmon." I read the description from the menu aloud. "Salmon steak wrapped in prosciutto, topped with mozzarella cheese and a sweet balsam-ic reduction. Served with sautéed spinach with grape toma-toes and garlic-mashed potatoes. This one's for me. Prosciutto reminds me of Italy. Jon and I were there last November," I said for Candy and Bo's benefit and to steer the topic away from Patsy's death. "The most marvelous place on this earth, outside of home."

Italy was where Jon had proposed.

"I agree," Bo said. "Candy and I were there last summer. We can't wait to go back."

Bo was a husky guy with spiky white blonde hair. Kind of an aging surfer type. I wondered if he still surfed. I knew from Jon that he dived.

"My friend and I took his boat out this morning and dived off Southport. He knows just where the *Kate* is sunk. Gee, that was exciting, to swim around the remains of that old steamer. She was one of the blockade runners, you know."

"Jon and I have discovered her too," Cam said. "She's got a bad reputation, did you know?"

"Well, sure," Bo said. "I know all about the blockade runners."

"Then you know it was the *Kate* that brought the Yellow Fever epidemic to Wilmington," Cam said.

"Well . . ." Bo didn't look too sure of himself. It's a man thing, this need to one up the next guy. But he confessed, "Actually, no, I didn't know that. Guess I was out partying the day they covered that one in class. So what's the story?"

"Sailors on board the *Kate* were infected with Yellow Fever and brought it to Wilmington. Later, when the authorities figured out how the disease was transmitted, they quarantined all ships before allowing them into port," Jon explained. "Yellow Jack wiped out fifteen percent of Wilmington's population," he added.

Cam said, "A few months later, the *Kate* was making another run into Wilmington. She had just crossed the Western bar at Old Inlet when she hit an obstruction in the Cape Fear and sank. Jon and I like to go down and swim around what's left of her. Kind of eerie."

Melanie looked at Cam with pride. "And how do you know all that, my California boy?"

Cam beamed, the way he does when Melanie lavishes affection on him. He is so transparent. "I've been reading up on local history. Might make a good documentary."

Not to be one-upped, Bo said with a chuckle, "By the way, did you know that this guarding of the sand bar stuff is where the term 'bartender' originated. Ha, isn't that a good one?"

He continued, "I understand there was nothing left on board the *Kate* when she went down. According to my friend, the cargo was salvaged before she sank. Wonder if she was carrying gold for the Confederacy? Gold from the sale of cotton and tobacco, you know, intended for the Confederate army. That's how they paid the soldiers, when they could: half gold, half Confederate currency." He kind of grimaced. "And everyone knows the fate of Confederate currency."

"You hoping to find gold?" Cam asked.

"Sure. Doesn't everyone who dives?"

"If you did find it, it would belong to the state," Jon said. "Anything found within the three mile limit belongs to the state. So it wouldn't do you any good. Maybe get you a write-up in the paper. Your fifteen minutes of fame." He grinned.

Jon has a grin that makes me want to throw my arms around him and kiss him.

Bo shrugged indifferently. "Well, sure, I guess if you were sucker enough to report that you'd found gold. If you've got a big mouth. But keep your discovery to yourself, and you get to keep the gold." He lowered his sunglasses and gave Candy a wink. Like her, he seemed very sure of himself.

Melanie stuck a pin in his balloon. "There isn't any gold down there."

"Sure there is," Bo argued.

"No, there isn't," I said. You couldn't be a good friend of

Binkie's and not know a few facts about local history. I went on to explain, "When a blockade runner was sinking, the first thing the sailors did was save the cargo. And the first cargo to be put onto a launch and sent ashore was gold. You have to remember, those sailors were paid in gold. They were not part of the military; they were mostly privateers. Why, the blockade runners were not even armed. They never shot back when attacked by a Union Navy vessel. To do so would have got them a death sentence.

"They carried the gold in kegs, like beer. Heavy, but it would go into the launch and they'd sail it over to Ft. Fisher or Federal Point or Smithville. Do you think they'd let the Union Navy get their hands on that gold? Those sailors would die first."

"But," Bo argued, "maybe they'd sink it first too. And it's still down there if you know where to look."

"OK, fellas, the only gold that interests me is the kind I can buy at Tiffany's. Let's order. I'm with Ashley, I'm starved."

And we all laughed and Bo signaled to the waiter. But he got a dreamy expression on his face, and said, "Nineteenth century gold sovereigns are more valuable than watered-down Tiffany's gold."

15

I gave Binkie a hug and kiss. He is so cute. No wonder Aunt Ruby fell for him — twice.

After we had finished eating dinner, Melanie had dashed back to speak to the special event planner about holding our bridesmaids' luncheon at the restaurant. "The Bridge Tender is Faye Brock's favorite restaurant," she'd told us. "And I've asked her to be a bridesmaid. So we'll hold the luncheon here to please her because she's such a sweetheart."

Then she left us and that gave me time to have dessert before she returned to whisk me away to Binkie's in her red Mercedes convertible. We kissed the boys goodnight and drove back to town. My car and my van were both parked downtown, my van still at the Captain's house. I'd pick it up later and drive out to Jon's for another night. As much as I love spending the night with him and as fond as I am of his house, I found myself longing to get back into my own home and felt impatience building. I wanted to get to work cleaning up the mess Patsy and Jimmy had left, and to experience the luxury of living in my own space with my own possessions again.

On the drive, something alarming occurred to me. "Melanie!" I screeched.

"What!" she screeched back and her hands flew off the steering wheel and she slammed on the brake.

"Watch your driving!" I exclaimed.

"Well, what's wrong," and she turned to fix me with a glare. This was hopeless.

"If you don't focus on your driving, I'm going to insist that you pull off so I can take the wheel."

Melanie arched her eyebrows. "Nobody drives this baby but me." Melanie was always having a love affair with her latest car. And sometimes I was just as bad.

"Melanie," I began again, "Jimmy Pogue has the keys to my house. Remember? You gave them to him."

"Oh my gosh, you're right. We'll get the locks changed. As soon as those goofy police let us in, we'll call a locksmith."

Binkie was happy to see Melanie and me and invited us into the study where Aunt Ruby was settled comfortably. She had on a dress and looked pretty. Aunt Ruby was in her seventies but she colored her hair and laced up her Reeboks every day for a long walk around the district. A tray with iced tea and oatmeal cookies awaited us, and the air conditioner hummed quietly and coolly. The furnishings were old-fashioned, the very same furnishings Mrs. Higgins, Binkie's mother, had brought to her home as a bride in the early thirties. The style was the timeless English Country look with fat club chairs upholstered in a faded floral fabric with roses. A beautiful Chippendale breakfront filled one wall, with leather-bound books arranged behind glass doors. Aunt Ruby presided over a lovely mahogany tea table.

"The iced tea is decaffeinated," she said.

"We've just returned from a long walk around the historic district," Binkie told us. "Everywhere we went, they were talking about Patsy Pogue being murdered in your gazebo. And the police cars are still at your house." "Now, you girls sit down and make yourselves at home," Aunt Ruby said. "Ashley, sweetie, you've had yourself a trying day from what I hear tell, now would you like something stronger than tea? We've got a lovely cream sherry that we haven't opened yet."

Binkie paced about. "How dreadful for you, Ashley, to find that writer killed that way. As upsetting as the murder at Two Sisters. I can't imagine what is happening to our town. It used to be so peaceful here."

"Sit down, Benjamin," Aunt Ruby said. "You're working yourself up to a nervous snit."

"Iced tea is fine, Aunt Ruby," Melanie said as she seated herself on a Chippendale sofa covered in soft, well-worn chintz.

"Ashley and I think Jimmy Pogue is behind these murders. We think he killed Patsy. Ashley overheard them quarreling about Captain Pettigrew's house. And we think he killed Hugh Mullins at Two Sisters. And . . ." she went on importantly, "we think Captain Pettigrew's journal might offer a clue as to the motive. Because the police are just not listening to us."

"Have you had time to study the journal, Binkie?" I asked.

He answered with a question of his own. "Patsy Pogue and her husband quarreled over Captain Pettigrew's house? I've never met the man. Never even heard of him. Or his wife."

And why would he? Binkie read scholarly books. He was not into novels.

Binkie folded his hands over his stomach. He shook his head as if puzzled. "I've read every entry in that journal, and while his narratives are a stupendous find from a military history perspective, I cannot find a clue to these current murders. There are accounts of his voyages as he delivered goods from the Southern States to Bermuda or to Liverpool, then sailed home from England with cargo for the Confederacy. He was consigned to various ships, some owned by mercantile shippers, others by the Confederacy. Many of the entries are nothing more than ships manifests, itemized lists of cargo. Let me show you."

He got up and went to the breakfront, opened a glass door and retrieved the journal. Then sitting down again, he opened the journal and read an entry.

July 1863 – Wilmington

Awaiting entry into the Wilmington Port. Another safe journey across the Atlantic on the CSS Gibraltar under the command of Captain E. C. Reid. Formerly the screw packet Sumter, she had been sold by the Confederacy to the Charleston shipping company of Fraser, Trenholm and Company, and sent to Liverpool for conversion to a merchantman. Then she was repurchased by the Confederacy so that she could transport a most important cargo. On July 3, we departed Liverpool with a pair of powerful 12.75-inch Blakely cannons, each weighing over 27 tons. The cannons are so huge it was impossible to conceal them from the British authorities. Ingenuously, Captain Reid devised a way to display them in full view yet to conceal them. The cannons were harnessed upright in vertical positions in the cargo hatches, disguised to look like extra smokestacks. The authorities were fooled.

Approaching the outer blockade of the Cape Fear, Captain Reid audaciously hoisted the Union flag and we slipped easily through the line. It wasn't until we were under the protection of the big guns at Ft. Fisher that the blockaders realized we were not one of their own. By then it was too late for them to give chase. I piloted the ship safely up the Cape Fear where we are now waiting out our term of quarantine before commencing to the port and home. The Captain has received word that the cannons are desired by none other than General Beauregard himself and are destined for the Charleston Battery.

"The entire journal is filled with such entries," Binkie

said. "This diary is a treasure. But try as I might, I cannot find anything that Captain Pettigrew has written that would be a motive for murder today."

"When did Thomas Pettigrew get promoted from a pilot to a Captain?" I wanted to know.

"That came later. Young Thomas experienced many adventures before he was given command of his own ship. For example, he sailed with Captain Holgate on the CSS *General Beauregard*'s final voyage. The *Beauregard* was run aground while under heavy fire from three blockaders. Knowing the jig was up, the Captain ordered the crew to open the sea cocks and flood the ship. He'd rather sink it than let the Union Navy get their hands on it.

"Captured blockade runners were sold in a prize court, and the crew that captured it received half of the proceeds. Then the Union would mount guns and convert the ship into a blockader.

"The crew of the *Beauregard* escaped and sailed to shore in small boats; some of the sailors swam to safety. None of the crew was lost, but wet and shivering they made their way to a river pilot's home.

"The wreck of the *General Beauregard* can still be seen off Carolina Beach during low tide."

"Cam told me he and Jon dive around that wreck," Melanie said. She gave a little shake. "I have no desire to dive underwater to see those spooky old sunken ships."

I got the impression that Cam had still not told Melanie of his accident with his diving gear. Jon said they were taking a break from diving, both of them busy with work, and that before their next diving venture they would have their gear checked out thoroughly and the faulty air-tubing replaced. I had said, "You'd better." For now, all diving adventures were on hold. And just as well, I thought.

Binkie went on. "To answer your question of when Thomas Pettigrew commanded his own ship, he writes about that in several entries. In the summer of 1864, he took command of his old friend, the *Gibraltar*. The ship was laid up for repairs at Birkenhead, England. But the British textile mill owners were desperate for our cotton and willing to pay dearly for it. So they formed a consortium with a small mercantile company and purchased the *Gibraltar*, hiring young Pettigrew to Captain it. He was an experienced seaman — brave and daring — and familiar with the ship. Plus, he was trustworthy. An ideal choice. His job was to deliver as much cotton as possible as quickly as possible to the consortium members. In exchange, the consortium would supply munitions, meats, uniforms, and gold to the Confederacy. And for his services he was well paid."

"If he was paid in gold," I speculated, "perhaps that is what is at the bottom of these murders. And perhaps the gold is hidden in the Captain's house and the murderer is trying to find it."

16

"But then why steal Binkie's briefcase?" Melanie argued.

"Because he thought the journal would tell where the gold was hidden," Aunt Ruby volunteered.

"But it doesn't," Binkie declared. "And I read every entry in that journal. There is no reference to anything being hidden in his house."

"But the killer doesn't know that, my love," Ruby said. "I want that journal out of here and fast."

"Yes, ma'am," Binkie said and gave her a little salute. "You and I will have one last perusal, and then it's off to the library's archives." He winked at Melanie and me.

I had been thinking. "According to Laura Gaston, Lacey lived on her brother's earnings for all of her life, and used what was left to set up a trust fund to care for the property when she was gone."

"And here's another thing," Melanie said, "if Jimmy Pogue is our killer and the motive is gold hidden in the Captain's house, why did Patsy tell him he should have burned the house down when he had the chance?"

"And why was he trying to remove the artifacts from the house when I caught him at it red-handed?"

"What did you do with that box of artifacts?" Melanie asked. Her green eyes were blazing with excitement.

"Jon and I went through everything. Believe me there was no gold in that box. Nor were there any letters or journals, just nineteenth-century objects, lanterns and such. I gave them to the Cape Fear Museum."

"Well, based on what we've learned, Ashley dear," Binkie said, "I believe you must take measures to ensure that the Captain's house is secure at all times. And you must instruct Willie Hudson not to admit anyone he does not know. Further, if there is a chance that Jimmy Pogue may want to set fire to the house, you should hire a night watchman as well."

It was fully dark at ten o'clock when Melanie drove me to the Captain's house on Front Street so that I could pick up my van. We sat in her car for a moment. The convertible's top was down and the night was hot, but it was a pleasant heat — the heat of a Southern summer night. I love the summer. I love the sultry breezes that waft off the Cape Fear to caress my skin and curl my hair.

The windows were now completely installed in the Captain's house and inky blackness showed from within. But with white primer on the house, it seemed illuminated. Ambient city light glowed all around us, and the bright lights from Chandler's Wharf below flickered through the trees. Out on the river, Memorial Bridge spanned the water like a sparkling diamond necklace stretched out on dark blue velvet.

"Kind of spooky, isn't it?" I said about the Captain's house, and before the words were out of my mouth, I saw a light flash from one of the upstairs rooms.

"Did you see that?" I asked Melanie.

"See what?"

"That flash of light. Someone is in the house! Binkie was right."

Melanie looked where I pointed. "I don't see anything."

"It was just there. A flash of light, like from a flashlight."

"Could have been a reflection of car headlights passing by," she said. "Binkie has got your imagination fired up."

"Don't start with me, Melanie. I know what I saw. There! There it is again." A light flickered through the window of the second floor front room, then disappeared.

"I saw it too," Melanie said in an awed voice. "Do you have your keys? Come on. Let's go inside and catch whoever it is."

"No way! I don't want us to be the murderer's next victims."

"I'm not afraid to confront that wimpy Jimmy Pogue. He's a coward. The way he murdered those people was cowardly. Sneaking up from behind and reaching around and stabbing them. Only a coward would kill that way. No eye contact."

"Since when have you become an expert on murderers' MOs? There is no way I am going into that house, or that I'll let you go in either."

"Oh, pish posh. I guess you're right. But we said we wanted to solve this crime on our own."

"Look, Melanie, just because we've got a red roadster, doesn't mean we are Nancy Drew and Bess." I whipped out my cell phone and dialed 911, reported a prowler, and gave the dispatcher the address. I was calling 911 much too often these days. I had to get a life — a normal life. I should be planning my wedding, instead I was sitting on the street with Nancy Drew in her red convertible in River Heights, waiting for the police to arrive once again.

It must have been a slow night for Wilmington PD or else the address on Front Street had been input into their computers with bells and whistles attached, because in five minutes a patrol car arrived. During that time neither Melanie nor I had seen a flicker of light within the house. "He's gone," I said, disappointed. "He spotted us out here and left the same way he got in."

Melanie and I got out of the convertible and stood on the sidewalk. A uniformed police officer stepped from the driver's side of the patrol car. But when I saw who got out of the passenger side, my mouth fell open and I felt like I had been punched in the gut. Nick!

"What . . . what are you doing here, Nick?" Then I blabbered nervously. "I heard you were back. Diane said you were after your old job. Did they hire you back? Are you on the force again?"

Nick doesn't get flustered the way I do. He was the personification of Mr. Cool himself. "It's a quiet night. I'm just here on a ride-along," he said casually, as if it was no big deal that he was riding in a patrol car on a call about a break-in that involved his estranged wife.

Nick was much too cool and controlled to ever have been right for me. Jon's every feeling showed on his face and he didn't try to suppress his emotions. He never hid from me behind a façade of indifference.

"Give me your keys," Nick instructed and stretched out his hand.

I deposited the heavy key ring in his upturned palm. He handed the keys to the uniformed officer. "I'll just have a walk around out here." He disappeared into the darkness of the sloping side yard, while the officer used the keys to open the door. I ran up behind him. "I'll show you how to turn on the lights."

Melanie was barking up my shins in her haste. "Stop stepping on my heels," I howled.

The officer turned back to us with a menacing, "Keep it down."

After I turned on the strings of glaring bare-bulb work lights, we moved into the reception hall. "You ladies wait out in your car," the officer told us, and groaning with disappointment Melanie led the way back out into the street.

"Oh pooh. I hate it that we can't get in on the action. I really like this detective stuff," she told me with a frown.

Get in on the action? A few turns at finding dead bodies and she'd be cured.

Nick and the officer returned together, huddling and speaking in low tones. Then they came over to us. "Rogers, this is my wife, Ashley Wilkes. And that is her sister, Melanie Wilkes. This is Officer Rogers, an old friend."

"Ex-wife," I corrected.

"Not yet," Nick said, and I did a double take. I faced the two of them squarely and said in a firm voice, "We are separated. Our divorce will be final in December." Then I gave Nick a menacing look of my own, as if to say: What's your problem?

Officer Rogers said, "I know who you are, Miss Wilkes. Everybody does. Your reputation precedes you, as they say. Now, ladies, I checked the entire house and there was no one in there. But Nick found a raised first floor window on the side yard. Probably just a curiosity seeker poking around, nothing better to do. I didn't see any signs of damage but with all the construction going on, it's hard to tell."

Nick was walking to his side of the patrol car. "Better tell your workers to lock up when they leave," he advised smugly.

"Wait a minute. Wait a minute," I called. "This has something to . . ."

Melanie grabbed my hand and pulled me back. "No," she hissed. "Don't involve him."

But I broke away and caught up with Nick. "Tell me one thing," I said. "You owe me. Did the police find prints on the knife handles?"

He gave me a thoughtful look, as if weighing what he might owe me. "Yes, they got good prints. Trouble is, they don't match any prints on file. Not everybody gets finger-printed, you know."

He opened the car door. Anticipating my next question, he said, "Same prints on both knives."

17

Close to midnight I slid into bed beside Jon. He did not awake, but in his sleep became aware of my presence for he reached out his arms to enfold me. I moved into his embrace and listened to his quiet breathing. I experienced deep contentment and felt secure. My encounter with Nick had shaken me, had caused all the old insecurities I'd experienced when married to him to surface. I was so glad to get back to the safety of my precious Jon.

As my body eased into relaxation, my mind raced. What a day! Finding Patsy, the police, selecting my wedding gown, dinner with the gang and Candy and Bo, Captain Pettigrew's journal, the prowler in the Captain's house, the police again. And finally seeing Nick for the first time since last November.

I'd never be able to sleep. But I did. I decided to focus my thoughts on the wedding gown, pictured myself walking down the aisle with Melanie — Jon and Cam waiting at the altar. I smiled to myself and drifted off. There were better days ahead.

At some point during the night I awoke briefly, reminding myself that I had to make a thorough search of the Captain's house.

And so the next morning, Friday, after a hearty breakfast with Jon at the Causeway Café on Harbour Island during which I filled him in on last night's prowler, we were back at work at the Captain's house. The din of hammering on the exterior was horrific as carpenters completed the job of replacing rotting wood with new on the south wall. As Jon and Willie Hudson engaged in a shouted consultation about the break-in last night, my mind skipped ahead to possible hiding places. I'd start upstairs first.

Willie said he was sure he had locked up last night but would double check from now on, and told us his grandson Dwayne was looking for work, and a night shift would suit him fine. Dwayne was on summer break from UNCW, and worked as a bouncer at a downtown club on Saturday nights.

"He's on the wrestling team at the college. He's got the experience, and he's big and sassy."

"Like his grandpa," I joked.

Willie Hudson was an admirable man, a leader in his church and in the black community, and his extended family numbered in the legions. I counted him as a friend, and in fact, Jon had asked him to be one of the groomsmen at our wedding. Willie's response had been, "You want an old guy like me?"

Jon had replied, "Ashley and I can't get married without you in the wedding party. You are one of our best friends. Besides, we may need a bouncer at the wedding. Who knows how many of Melanie's old lovers will show up? And when the minister asks, does anyone here know of a reason why these two cannot be wed, he may just get a chorus of yeses."

I began my search in the room Laura Gaston had told me had been Lacey's room when she was a little girl. The second floor had been built under the eaves with a minimum of attic space overhead. Lacey's room had dormer windows and sloping walls. Where would a little girl hide letters, I asked myself.

Antebellum houses did not have closets as we know closets to be today, but they did have cupboards fitted into spaces that otherwise would have been dead space. There were tiny cupboards tucked in under the dormer windows in Lacey's room, but as I opened the knee-high doors and crouched down to look inside, I found nothing but dust bunnies. On her last trip to Wilmington, Laura had told me that when she was in medical school and after her father's hit-and-run accident that forced him to move out of the house, she spent her free time sorting through generations of accumulated household and personal items, putting some in storage, disposing of others. Items of sentimental and historical value, like the Captain's journal, she had taken with her to New York.

Laura was engaged to a coast guard officer stationed in Wilmington. They were conducting a long-distance romance but would soon live in the same town. I was eager for Laura to return again so that I could ask her many questions. But she was attending a conference of orthopedic surgeons in Toronto and would not return to Wilmington until next week. Until then, I was on my own.

Next, I crawled along the floor looking for loose floorboards. The space under a floor board would make a dandy hiding place. Unlike the floor downstairs, the second floor was in good condition and I could only assume it was because of all of the warmth and sunlight the top of the house captured during our long summers. Old houses and how they age are a mystery. No one knows precisely why one section holds up and another falls apart.

This was the room where I'd seen the flashing light last night. This room, and the adjoining room. So someone else had been up here searching, looking for another letter from Captain Pettigrew or another journal. The prowler knew what he was looking for; I did not.

Crawling along I did encounter a loose floor board. And from the looks of it — marks along the edges, disturbed dust

— the prowler had beaten me to it. Prying the board up with the tip of a screw driver, I saw only an empty space between it and the sub-flooring. Empty and dirty. There were no ghost marks of an object having been hidden here, and no smears in the dirt from someone pawing around inside. Nothing.

I was poking around in the next room when Jon came up the stairs. He looked troubled. Something was wrong, his expression told me. "Ashley, Nick's downstairs. He wants to talk to you."

"Well, I don't want to talk to him," I said. I had no desire to rehash our marriage and our breakup. I was happy these days. Why relive a failed marriage? I wasn't a masochist. Then I had a second thought. Perhaps this had nothing to do with us. Perhaps he wanted to talk to me about the murders. "Oh, maybe it's about the break-in last night. All right, I'll talk to him."

At my first sight of him, I felt nothing. And for that I was grateful. There was a time when just the sight of him took my breath away. Now that reaction was gone, and I knew I was completely over him. During the course of our separation I had wondered if some bit of passion might still be lingering. But that was not so. I felt nothing, only sadness for the failure. I don't like failure. Those who love me tell me I am too hard on myself, and perhaps they are right. I was born with a Jiminy Cricket conscience. Melanie was not. A part of me wished I could sail blithesomely through life as Melanie did, with little regard for the consequences of my actions and the broken hearts I'd left in my wake.

"Hello, Ashley," Nick said solemnly. "I thought we could take a walk. I have something to tell you."

So this *was* about the murders, I thought.

We strolled down the hill toward the river in awkward silence. What was he waiting for, I wondered. I decided to start the conversation since he was not. "What have the police learned about Hugh Mullins?" I asked.

"Hmmmm? Oh, Mullins. The vic." He gave me a pointed look. Nosy as usual, that look said. "He's from London. Here on vacation. Traveling along the East Coast. And somehow got invited by Melanie to the investors' weekend she hosted. She probably knows as much about him as the police do."

"No. No, she doesn't. He got in touch with her and told her he was interested in acquiring a house in Wilmington. That he planned to spend part of the year here. She had room for one more in her group, so she told him to come along."

We stepped onto Riverwalk at the foot of Ann Street. Morning sunlight glinted off the water and I put on my dark glasses. The air still retained a hint of morning freshness, but in an hour that would be gone, burnt off by the sun.

We shared the wooden boardwalk that bordered the river with strollers and joggers and dogs on leashes. Still Nick did not initiate a conversation, and I began to wonder what this was about. He was thinner than the last time I had seen him, looking almost gaunt. And he seemed weary, defeated.

"Do you have information about the murders?" I asked, reminding him that it was he who had called this meeting.

"The murders? No. Ashley, I want to talk about us." He paused for a moment and regarded me intently. As was his habit, he was immaculately dressed in a summer weight tailored suit. Nick had always dressed beautifully.

"I'd rather not talk about us," I said, and began to walk swiftly and furiously. In a few long strides he caught up. With a gentle touch on my arm, he stopped me. By then, we had reached Riverfront Park at Water and Market streets.

"Let's sit down," he suggested and led me to a bench on the promenade that overlooked the river. Behind us loomed the Alton Lennon Federal Building, which in the *Matlock* series had been portrayed as Matlock's court house. The Henrietta III was docked at the foot of Dock Street where tourists lined up for the river cruise. Across the river, the mighty World War II battleship *North Carolina* was tethered and anchored, another tourist attraction.

Nick sat hunched forward, his elbows on his knees, his hands ready to spring into action, to help him explain himself to me. For now I realized that was what was coming. His head was turned toward me, taking me in fully. I could feel myself growing twitchy as I repressed the urge to jump up and run. I did not want to hear this.

He took a deep breath and began. "Everything you've thought about me was right, Ashley. I see that now. I really let you down. I let us down. You came into my life too soon, that was the problem. I wasn't ready to experience the love of my life. I had my life planned out. First my career. Then later when I was established, I'd have time to fall in love. Not now."

He looked at me despairingly. "But my heart had other ideas. That first year, when we were dating, I could feel myself growing close to you and the feeling terrified me." His hands sprang into action.

"I had my plans all laid out. Build up a solid career first. Then find someone and get married. But you came along and you are not the kind of woman a man uses for a casual fling. You are the kind of woman a man marries."

I stilled my body and I stilled my mind. I didn't say a word. Didn't want to interrupt the flow of his confession. On some level I think I knew all this. I knew these things about myself. I had never been capable of Melanie's "the grass is always greener" approach to romance. If only Nick had opened up to me while we were married, we might have . . . What?

He went on. "That first year, while we were dating, I tried to forget you by joining Atlanta PD's cold case task force. I thought if I put some distance between us, I'd meet someone else, you'd meet someone else, and I could continue with my game plan. But it didn't work out that way. I tried not returning your calls, not answering your emails. But I couldn't forget you. So I came back."

He held up a palm, forestalling my protest. "Oh, I know. You thought I came back because Wilmington PD had offered me the Homeland Security liaison position. Well, yes, that was a part of my decision. But the main reason I returned to Wilmington was to be near you, to resume our love affair."

He shook his head as if to reaffirm his words. "It was never just dating, Ashley, it was a love affair from Day One. Was for me, anyway. The first time I saw you in that dusty old house, dirty and sweaty and covered with plaster dust, I still saw who you were. I recognized you instantly as the love of my life."

He looked down at his feet. "So there, now you know how I've always felt about you. Do I have a chance?" He reached over and took my hand. "Do we have to get this divorce? Can't we work this out?"

"Oh, this is so unfair, Nick. You are the one who kept leaving. You were always traveling for Homeland Security. And then you told me you were going to Quantico and instead you went off to Iraq. And I didn't even know you were out of the country. I had the best news for us: that we were expecting a baby and I couldn't find you to tell you. No one knew where you were."

He started to say something but I pushed his hand away. "Oh, I know, military wives go through this all of the time. But I never signed on to be a military wife, Nick. You lied to me about what you were doing. I didn't have a clue about which organization you were working for: the CIA, Blackwater? I still don't know. Don't want to know now. You never gave me the choice of becoming a brave military wife. At least those women get to send emails to their husbands."

He started to say something. "No, don't interrupt. You started this. Now you are going to hear me out. When I lost our baby and you weren't there to grieve with me, to help me through it . . . well, I just thought, if I can make it through the dreadful experiences of my life without Nick — losing my mother, losing my baby — then do I really want him around for the happy times? And the answer was no."

I started to say something about how Jon had stood by me, but decided that wasn't a wise course. Leave Jon out of this.

"But the straw that broke the camel's back was your having an affair with that Blackwater Security woman. And your joining that dreadful mercenary outfit. How could you?"

He had the decency to look contrite. "I really learned my lesson about that one, Ashley. I've learned a lot in the past six months. Doesn't that mean that it's not too late for me?"

When I did not reply, he went on, hoping to convince me. "Going to Iraq was such a mistake. The invasion of Iraq was the policy error of the century. You can't imagine what I saw firsthand." His eyes got a haunted look as he remembered.

"It's anarchy over there. In Ramadi, where I was assigned, they get electricity for two hours out of every twenty-four. And the temperatures are well over a hundred degrees. The Marines go on twelve day rotations and when they are on rotation they live in a fortress. You can't imagine how bad the conditions are for them. They have no bathrooms so no showers. They have to defecate into plastic bags, then burn their garbage. And when they go out into the courtyard to burn stuff, they are sitting ducks for rooftop snipers. The most dangerous time is when they go out on patrol. Because there is no garbage collection, the streets are filled with garbage, and that provides the insurgents with hiding places for IEDs. They are hidden everywhere, in the carcasses of dead animals . . . everywhere."

He shook his head in consternation. "When the Marines patrol a section of town and it's dead quiet, that's how they know there's a bomb waiting for them. Because the neighborhood has been tipped off and the residents flee the bomb. Or sometimes they are not tipped off and the innocents die — children playing in the street, women at the market, men looking for work. Dead."

He looked so sad, so beaten, that I reached out and took his hand again. "I'm sorry, Nick. It must have been awful for you. Awful for the ones still there, but that doesn't explain the infidelity."

Abruptly, he stood up. "You're right. There is no excuse. That was just me running away from my feelings again. I thought if I could throw myself into a dispassionate affair, I could get back control of my emotions."

He took my hand and pulled me up, looked me fully in the face. "Please remove your dark glasses. I want to be able to see your eyes."

I did as he asked.

"Ashley, I am truly sorry I hurt you. If you can find it in your heart to forgive me, if you can take me back, I promise you things will be different. I'm getting my old job back with the PD here. I'll settle down. No more double shifts. I'll concentrate on us, our marriage, our home. We'll have another baby."

Up until then I had been softening. But that did it. "You talk about having babies as if they are interchangeable, Nick. I only knew ours for a couple of months but already I loved it. You can't have a baby to replace the one you lost. Besides, I don't think I'm capable of having children."

He grabbed me then and held onto me fiercely. "That's doesn't matter. I only want you. If we can't have kids, that's OK too. But I want you. I need you."

The searing pain I experienced felt like my heart was being ripped out. "I can't, Nick. I'm sorry, but I can't. It's too late. It's over. I'm so sorry."

And with that I pulled out of his arms and ran. Tears blinded me so that I didn't see the wheelchair until I stumbled over it and was knocked to the hard wood decking of the promenade.

"Ashley, are you all right?" Nick cried, lifting me to my feet.

"Ashley?" another voice asked. "Are you injured, dear?"

The man in the wheel chair was Clarence Gaston, Laura Gaston's father.

"Mr. Gaston," I said. "I'm OK." I looked down to see skinned knees, just like a seven year old. "Did I hurt you when I ran into you?"

"Oh, no, I'm quite fine," he replied. "My steel chariot here protects me." And he smiled ruefully at his reference to his wheel chair.

The nurse behind the wheel chair said hello.

"You're just fine, Mr. Clarence. Just fine. No harm done," she said. "But this young lady, she has skinned up those pretty knees, just like one of my grandchildren."

I swiped at my knees. "I'll just go home and paint them with Mercurochrome then," I joked.

Nick was looking at us, wondering how we knew each other. I explained who Mr. Gaston was. Then told him, "We're making good progress on the house, Mr. Gaston."

"Oh, I know that, young lady. I'm keeping tabs on you and on it. I do get out some, even for a crippled man. And I'm sorry your life has become so unpleasantly eventful recently. Let's just hope the police can get to the bottom of these crimes. I don't have a whole lot of confidence in them, unfortunately. They never did find out who ran me down. Ran me down and left me for dead," he said bitterly.

The nurse said, "Now Mr. Clarence, don't you go getting

yourself worked up over that. What's done is done. And you know better. Now let's let this young woman go home and attend to those knees, and you and me are going to finish our stroll. Then it's time for lunch, and have I got a lunch planned for you. We'll be having . . ."

With a cordial wave of a hand, she started off, the wheel chair in front of her, her patient influenced by her good nature. If I ever got sick, I wanted a wise, caring nurse just like her.

Mr. Gaston turned his head and called, "My girl will be home next week. Home for good."

Nick took my elbow. "That nurse is right. We need to go to our house and wash those knees."

Our house? I let that one go by. "I can't," I said and felt frustrated and furious. "I can't get into my house." I emphasized the word "my." "Your old friend Diane Sherwood has made herself my worst nightmare and will not let me back into my house."

"I think I can do something about that," Nick said. "Let me take care of it."

18

The following Monday I was allowed to move back into my house. I'd spent a quiet and recuperative weekend with Jon, but by Monday I was champing at the bit to get home again. By then the kitchen smelled bad, really really bad. The food on the unwashed dishes had hardened, spoiled, and stank. The kitchen was filthy. If it were not for being so mad, I would have cried. Instead I pulled a large black plastic garbage bag from the box I'd purchased on my way home, and began to fill it, my fury giving me the endurance to confront Patsy's rotten food.

I dumped the plates in the bags along with the food. They were Patsy's fiesta ware and I wanted no part of them. All I wanted to do was purge my home of what I was coming to think of as "the Patsy karma." Spoiled food in the kitchen, her soiled clothes dumped on my bed, long gray hairs in my bathroom, face powder on my great-grandmother's rosewood dressing table, and dirty junk furniture in the parlor.

Where was Jimmy? If the police were looking for him, they had not confided that information to me. I had learned through Candy Murray, whom we'd had dinner with at Blue

Water on Saturday evening, that Patsy and Jimmy were not actually from Charlotte, but from Lincoln County. Was Jimmy hiding out there?

The black plastic garbage bags were lined up precisely along my curb like shiny soldiers. What must my neighbors think? I was in the process of setting out the seventh bag when the locksmith's truck pulled up. Within the hour I had new locks and new keys and as I have four outside doors to my first floor, I also had a sizeable hole in my checking account.

Melanie's cleaning crew arrived — three strong women who looked like they harbored a personal hatred for dirt and a love for the smell of cleaning products — and they set to work cleaning the entire house. Meanwhile, I continued to fill garbage bags with "pickins" from the parlor. The broken picture frames, the cracked crockery, a decades old faded flower arrangement. What in the world had Patsy intended to do with this trash?

The furniture was too large for me to move myself, but Jon, Cam, and Melanie were coming over at five and together we'd waltz the pieces out onto the porch and down to the curb. I just hoped the city would pick up everything without ticketing me. And that my neighbors would not get up a petition to have me banned from the street.

The cleaning women were incredible, moving with the speed of light, anxious to be on their way to someplace better. In their wake, they left the aroma of strong chemicals. I turned on ceiling fans and threw open windows.

But everything was nice and clean. In my bedroom, the bed had been made with fresh sheets, the comforter turned down neatly. Patsy's clothes had been loaded into plastic bags as I had requested. I picked up the bag with the idea of toting this too to the curb when something occurred to me. As much as I loathed touching her clothing, I opened the bag and dumped the articles of clothing out into the middle of the rug.

I went through the pockets of her clothing. Tortoise shell combs that she'd used to secure her long braid to the top of her head. A pale pink lipstick. Chocolate crumbs. Every tee shirt had a food stain but as they had no pockets I swiftly stuffed them back into the plastic garbage bag. Garbage to garbage, dust to dust.

Dust to dust? A funeral? Of course. Jimmy would have to return to Wilmington from wherever he was hiding. He would have to claim her body for burial. Would the police be waiting for him when he showed up?

And then in the pocket of a pair of size 18 jeans, I found something of interest. A tiny tape from a tape recorder. Hadn't Melanie said that Patsy wrote her books by speaking into a tape recorder? I wondered what was on the tape. I recalled that she had said she was onto a sensational story. Got me a humdinger of a plot for my next book, had been her exact words.

But I did not own a tape recorder that recorded on tapes. My tape recorder was the digital kind that recorded without a tape. I'd have to buy or borrow a tape recorder to find out what Patsy had been working on when she'd been routed from the *literati* forever.

And what did it matter? Did her next book have anything to do with her death?

I had brought a duffel bag full of dirty clothes with me from Jon's and as I spent the next couple of hours doing laundry I had time to think. The first thing I thought about was how grateful I was to be back in my own house. The second thing was how grateful I was that Patsy had been killed outside and not inside. Living in a house that was 147 years old, I had no expectation that there had never been a death in my house. In fact, I knew better. People had died here. And people had been killed here — murdered in my house. Those from the past I did not know. But two of my friends had been recent victims of homicide, and I grieved their passing. Patsy had not been a friend, to put it kindly, still it was a relief to me that she had not been murdered inside. How much worse would the Patsy karma have been if that were the case?

19

"I can't believe how colorful it is," Laura Gaston exclaimed. "I've seen old photos of the house, but those were in black and white. And you say these were the original colors?"

We were standing on Front Street directly in front of the Captain's house: Laura, her fiancé Jack Connelley, Jon, and I.

"The Victorians went in for exuberant colors," Jon said.

"We had scrapings of paint analyzed in a lab," I said. "The analysis revealed that the house had been painted this olive green, the window frames and sashes were a creamy white. The shutters were dark red, and trim work like the bullets were a bright yellow. Exactly what we will be applying soon."

The wood siding had been repaired, and the base coat had dried, allowing a crew of painters to begin the final painting.

I continued, "These front stairs are broad, so we will borrow a side section and that is where we will construct the ramp for the wheel chair."

"Daddy needs to have his room and bath on the first floor," Laura said.

"Yes, we know that," Jon said agreeably. "Come on inside and I'll show you what we are doing to accommodate your father and his needs." And he led the way across the porch and into the house. We moved to the rear parlor where the flooring had been replaced and felt good and solid under our feet. A plasterer was applying the last layer of plaster to the parlor walls. He said hello then went back to work.

"We've converted this back parlor into a bedroom for your dad. And by knocking through this wall," and he pointed to the addition, "and borrowing space from the kitchen side that used to be a pantry, we have made room for a bathroom. The doorways that he will be using will be wide enough to accommodate his wheelchair. The shower comes with a seat so he can have his shower sitting down. And the door opens in such a way to allow him to be transferred directly from his wheelchair into the shower, and out again."

"You've thought of everything," Jack Connelley said. Jack was a warrant officer at the Oak Island Coast Guard Station. The station conducted search and rescue missions, plus provided Homeland Security patrols. He and Laura had met at Ashley High School. They had been younger than Melanie and older than I, so neither of us knew them when we were teens.

Laura was a large-boned but spare woman with black wavy hair, a crisp no-nonsense manner — must be her doctor's training, I assumed — but was basically a kind person.

Jack was her opposite in looks. He appeared round, although there wasn't an ounce of fat on him. His face was round, and his glasses were round. And all the freckles on his face and arms were round. With short orangey-red hair he seemed friendly and approachable. He was not dressed in a uniform but wore casual clothing.

Theirs had been a long distance romance for several years, with Laura in med school in New York, and Jack here at Oak Island.

"The stairs to the lower level were closed off, as you know," I said. "We had them opened and repaired so you can now access the lower level from within the house."

"When I was a kid we had a tenant renting out that space," Laura said, "so that was when the stairs were sealed off. Then later, the place was just too big for Daddy and me so we never bothered to take down the wall and reinstall the door."

I walked them into the kitchen and showed them the now accessible staircase.

"We have big plans for the lower level," Jon said. "Because your dad's room will be where the old parlor used to be, we are designing a combination den/media room for you down there. That is where you two can relax without disturbing your father."

"Oh, that is a wonderful idea," Laura said, evidently very pleased. "The house is really very spacious, we just need an efficient layout."

"We're building a guest suite on the lower level as well," Jon said. "And up on the second floor, you'll have a large master suite, with a bath, and dressing room, large closets, and an office."

"I can't thank you enough," Laura said. "For a while I thought we were going to lose this house, and I just hated that. I grew up here. Well, you know that. Granted the place was held together with Scotch tape, but we have so much personal history here." She slipped an arm around Jack's waist. "And then Jack stepped in and saved the day. Paid the taxes, and funded my last year of med school."

"And worth every penny," Jack said.

"Well, it has been a privilege for Jon and me to restore your house. So, Jack, I too am grateful to you for keeping the house in the Captain's family."

Jack's high color became even brighter. "It was the least I could do. Laura wanted us to live here and I want what Laura wants. Besides," and he wagged his shaggy red-blonde eyebrows at us, "there's gold hidden here, didn't you know? Gold sovereigns from the Civil War. Worth a fortune now."

After the tour of the house and getting Laura's approval for everything we were doing, we stood chatting for a while on the sidewalk. They, of course, wanted to discuss the murders.

"That must have been so awful for you, Ashley," Laura said.

"It was," I said. But I hoped to keep our discussion professional.

"I hear the motive for the man's murder was over the theft of Professor Higgins' briefcase," Jack said. "I heard that the killer was after the journal Laura had sent to him. I've read that journal many times myself when I've been at Laura's apartment in New York. There is nothing in it that I ever saw that was worth killing for."

"If anyone can ferret out the truth, it is Binkie," I said. "But Jack, I don't believe the police released the information about the stolen briefcase. How did you know about the role it played in Hugh Mullins' murder?" I asked.

"Oh, being in law enforcement myself, word gets around. You can't keep secrets in this town."

"That's true," Jon said. And extended his hand to shake theirs goodbye. Jon and I were on the same wavelength. He knew I did not want to start gossiping about the murders but wanted to keep our relationship with Laura and Jack on a professional level.

"Bye," I said. "Jon is going back to work, but I've got to run. I'm meeting my sister and Aunt Ruby to sample wedding cakes."

"Oh," Laura said. "Who is making your cake? I'm kind of out of the loop here but we've got our own wedding to plan soon. Can you recommend a baker?"

"Sure," I said. "Melanie's friend Elaine McDuff is a really good caterer and she is preparing all of the food for our wedding. I can recommend her without reservation. She just opened a bakery in Leland."

I drove home, changed out of work duds and into a skirt and knit top. I slipped my feet into sandals with thanks for the warm weather. I love wearing sandals and don't get much chance to do so. Construction boots are not very feminine but I can't work on a restoration site without them. A nail through the sole of a sandal would not be a pleasant experience.

I drove to Binkie's to pick up Aunt Ruby and the two of us left him to his books and papers in the study. He gave me a distracted wave.

"He's been pouring over James Sprunt's writings for days," Aunt Ruby said. "I'm glad for this respite. I can't get a word out of the man, unless it has to do with the blockade."

I glanced at the breakfront but did not see the journal inside the glass doors. "Where's the journal?" I asked in an unnecessary whisper. But I needn't have whispered. Binkie did not even look up, so engrossed was he in the writings of the river pilot.

"He's hidden it somewhere. Not even I know where it is. He says I'm safer if I don't know. I can't wait to get that journal out of our house."

"Yes, I can understand that." I linked my arm through hers and walked her to my car. "I hope you're hungry," I said, "because we're going to be sampling cake, and you know Melanie, she never does anything half way."

Elaine McDuff was an old friend of Melanie's who had allowed herself to grow plump and motherly looking, even though she was a widow and childless. But oh! could that woman cook. She ran a very successful catering business and Melanie used her for all her parties and business receptions. I did too. The new bakery in Leland was an extension of her services. Elaine met us at the door and introduced us to her pastry chef, then excused herself to see to things in the back. Celeste was an older woman who was a relative of Willie Hudson's, actually, and who knew her way around the cake pans. She was a wizard with cake flour and created flawless fondant. She had tiny cakes made up for us to sample.

"Oh, try this, Aunt Ruby," Melanie exclaimed. "It is divine. What are these flavors, Celeste, they are so subtle?"

Celeste beamed. "You are eating pear-vanilla cake and the filling is cinnamon-cappuccino cream and hazelnut nougat. My own creation. Here have a little of this nice champagne to wash it down."

"We don't want to get drunk," I laughed. "We have to drive back to town."

"I'll be sure to serve you some nice strong coffee before I let you set foot outside the door," Celeste said. "Now this is very popular for the bachelor's cake. My very own recipe. Double fudge chocolate. Everyone loves this cake."

We took delicate bites of each cake. "I believe I'd go with the pear-vanilla cake for the wedding cake," Aunt Ruby said.

"I think so too," Melanie said. I looked at her and thought I'd never seen her so happy, so in her element. She was going to be a beautiful bride. If only Mama and Daddy were here to see her. And me.

I turned away to hide my tears. But I couldn't hold them back. I'd opened up a flood gate of tears. A delayed reaction to the shock of finding two murder victims, my overwhelming joy that I would be marrying Jon, and that Melanie had finally realized wonderful Cam was the man for her. Plus, missing our parents so much.

Aunt Ruby and Melanie were both hugging me and the three of us stood there, locked in a hug, rocking and patting, and "there, there"-ing each other.

When we pulled apart, I started to laugh. Oh, what an emotional roller-coaster.

Celeste shook her head. "Happens every time. I don't know what it is about my cakes, but they always get the brides to bawling!"

Made sober by the strong coffee and glasses of water Celeste had pressed upon us, I drove Aunt Ruby home. Melanie had driven in her Mercedes, having a closing scheduled on the west side of town.

"Yoo hoo, Binkie! We're home," Aunt Ruby called as she unlocked their front door. "Can you stay for a while, dear?" she asked me. "We'll have some iced tea. You know how Binkie loves . . ."

Her voice trailed off. We had passed through the entry hall and into the parlor. Seeing the overturned furniture and crashed lamps at the same time, we both screamed.
"Binkie!" Aunt Ruby shouted.

A disheveled Binkie came from the bathroom. He was holding an ice pack to his left temple.

"I'm all right, I'm all right," he said quickly. "Sit down, Ruby, you look like you might faint."

I helped Aunt Ruby to a chair, and she almost collapsed into it.

"What . . . what happened?"

"He came after you, didn't he?" I asked. "Looking for that journal."

"But he didn't get it," Binkie crowed. He was so proud of himself. "I gave as good as I got even if he was a young fellow. Landed my good right punch on his chin, and that man had to crawl to the door."

"Shall I take you to the hospital?" I asked. "Did you call the police?"

Binkie sat down on the arm of Ruby's chair and took her

hand. "Don't look so scared, love. I can take care of myself. You, too. He won't be coming back here again."

"But how did he get in?" she asked.

Binkie hesitated. "I let him in. The doorbell rang. I was distracted by my reading, so like a big fool I just absent-mindedly opened the door. He demanded the journal and when I said no, he took a swing at me. Well, that young punk didn't know that I've been training for this moment all of my life. I really gave it to him. Like I said, he had to crawl out of the door. Then he staggered to his feet and limped down the street."

"Did you recognize him?" I asked.

"Never saw him before. He looked like anybody you'd meet on the street, very average looking. Big shirt and droopy trousers like they wear these days. Hair covered by a ball cap. Dark glasses."

"I'll call the police," I said.

"Yes," Binkie agreed, "we'd better report this."

"I want that journal out of here," Aunt Ruby said in a scared voice.

"Soon, my love. Soon."

20

On Saturday afternoon the carpenter arrived at the Captain's house with the restored stair railing. He carried it in two sections and made additional trips to his truck to bring in the newel posts. Because the stairs turned at a ninety degree angle, the railing did not come as one continuous length.

"Oh, it looks beautiful," I exclaimed. "You hand stripped the old paint, didn't you?"

Sandy was an older gentleman who took pride in his work and had very fine manners. "Yes, ma'am, I never use chemical strippers. I've got small tools designed to fit the intricate detailing and I use the proper tool for the job. Then I sanded and stained the wood, three coats."

"Well, it looks fabulous," I said, clapping my hands together in applause.

"Before I install the railings, I'm going to repair these stairs for you. Like we talked about, you've got some loose risers. I constructed new treads at the shop for the ones that are broken. There are only a few. I'll remove the old, nail down the new, and sand and stain the stairs. Tomorrow, I'll come back and install the railings and give everything a finish coat."

Willie Hudson never worked on a Sunday, but Sandy was an independent craftsman and if he wanted to give up his Sunday to return to the house to finish the job, that was his business, I figured. Thanks to Willie having many grandsons of college age, we now had security personnel posted at the house when it was unoccupied so there would be someone here tomorrow to let Sandy inside.

While Sandy went to work on the stairs, I tackled the cleaning of the glass tiles on the fireplace surround. A new hearth had been laid to resemble the old, in jewel tone tiles to match the surround. Drab, indeed! The Victorians loved vibrant colors. Lovingly, I washed each individual tile with spray glass cleaner, rubbing and rubbing, until I brought it back to life. Melanie was picking me up at four and she would be appalled that I was dirty and smelled of ammonia but that couldn't be helped.

"Well, look at this, Miss Wilkes. Looks like someone used the inside of this step as a treasure box."

I had poured liquid hand sanitizer into my palm and was rubbing my hands together when his words brought me up short.

"Have you found something?" I asked excitedly.

Sandy withdrew a child's doll, delicate but grimy. I climbed the stairs and took it from him. "This must have belonged to Lacey, the Captain's little sister."

The doll's head, arms, and legs were made of bisque and were intact. Lacey had taken good care of her favorite dolly. But sawdust leaked from the seams of the doll's soft body. Under all the dirt and grim, her dress was made of black cloth, clumsily sewn. Lacey had made it herself, I guessed. But why black?

"Do you suppose the little girl was burying it here? A sort of coffin?" Sandy asked.

"I think you've hit upon it," I replied. "Children do play funeral. I remember burying dead birds in my parents' garden.

Is there anything else?" I asked expectantly.

Sandy bent his head and peered into the space under the tread. "Some papers."

He withdrew a crumbled dusty sheet of paper and handed it to me. I blew the dust away and was able to decipher, written in a childish hand, the words, *Thomas is dead*.

"Oh, no," I exclaimed.

Sandy turned to study me. "What is it, Miss Wilkes?"

"The note says, Thomas is dead. You know, Captain Pettigrew. Is there anything else?"

"Yes, pushed here at the back." And he reached in and pulled out an envelope.

He gave the envelope to me and I could scarcely breathe. By now I knew the Captain's handwriting and this writing was his. The envelope was addressed to Mrs. Jessica Pettigrew, his mother, at this address on Front Street.

"Uhhh," I breathed. "It's never been opened."

"Do you think it's important?" Sandy asked.

"Very important," I told him. To myself I said, It's the answer. The answer we've been searching for.

Just then the blare of car horns honking furiously came from the street. Sandy was nearest to the clerestory window and he stepped up to the landing and peered out over the porch roof. "It's your sister in a bright red convertible. And she's got traffic backed up behind her."

"Oh, my gosh. Melanie! She told me to be ready at four." Grasping the letter, I made a dash for the front door, picked up my purse which was sitting on the floor there, and hurried across the sidewalk to my impatient sister.

I had barely closed the car door and had not yet fastened my seat belt when she accelerated. Traffic behind us was backed up and the drivers were furious. "I thought we agreed you were going to be waiting out front for me at four o'clock. I declare, Ashley, you are the only woman I know who would be late for her final wedding dress fitting. And look at you, you're dirty!"

She cut across Nun Street, passed my house, and pulled into traffic on Third.

"Something important happened," I began. "We . . ."

"Something important is always happening at one of your houses. This is our wedding we're planning, for pity sakes," she lectured. "And knowing you, you'll probably be late for that!"

She raced out Dawson. "Do you have a nail file?" I asked.

She gave me a look of approval. I didn't say, Watch the road. What was the use?

"In my purse. On the floor. At least you're interested in nail care."

I rooted around in her purse and found a nail file at the bottom. Jeez, she had everything in that purse. No wonder it weighed a ton.

"Melanie," I said clearly and emphatically, "we found a letter from the Captain."

"You did!" she squealed, and her tires echoed the squeal as she sped onto Oleander. "Well, tell me quick. What did it say?"

"It's never been opened. That's why I asked for your nail file. I'm going to open it now." And with that I slit the envelope and removed the letter.

"Hold onto that thing," Melanie shouted. "You don't want it blowing away in the wind. We'll never find it."

"I'm holding on," I answered defensively.

"Well, read it then. What are you waiting for?"

And I read.

Dearest Mother,

I know you have been worried about me as I did not return home from my last voyage. There was much confusion in the fracas at Ft. Fisher that you have, no doubt, not been informed as to what befell the Gibraltar and her crew.

I don't want you worrying, Mother, but we were taken prisoner and are being held at Point Lookout prison in Maryland.

"Oh, no," I interjected.

"Don't stop. Read on," Melanie said. "Look, I'm afraid the wind is going to blow those pages right out of your hand so I'm pulling off into Belk's parking lot. This deserves my full attention." She parked and even managed to find a scrawny tree at the edge of the lot which offered a bit of shade.

I continued reading.

You will have heard horror stories about the prison, Mother, but let me assure you things are not too bad.

"Oh, what a sweet son," I said. "He's trying to reassure her. You know those Civil War prisons were hell holes, for both sides."

We are situated on the Chesapeake Bay, thus the sight of water lifts my spirits. You know I have the sea in my blood. The good local Quaker brothers tour our prison, bringing us food when they are able, and do their best to make our lives bearable. I have smuggled this letter to one of them who assures me he will be traveling South shortly and he has given me his word that he will place this missive directly into your hands as speedily as the Lord is willing.

I must tell you the tale of how I came to be in this place. We set sail from Liverpool in December with cargo urgently needed by the Confederacy. I was greatly disappointed that we would not make it home in time for Christmas as I had hoped. For weeks, we were out of communication as we crossed the Atlantic. Imagine our horror and surprise to arrive at the mouth of the Cape Fear and find Ft. Fisher under siege. A mighty armada of Union ships lay off the seaward side of the fort. All was quiet, but as we stealthily approached their rear, the assault on the fort began. The weather was mild, the day bright and balmy with calm winds, feeling like Indian summer. The barrage from the warships was continuous, filling our ears with a deafening roar and the air with the smoke of gunpowder. The smoke provided us with cover so that we were not seen by the warships.

We had two options open to us: retreat to Bermuda or try for home. As the Captain, the decision was mine, but I encouraged the men to vote on the matter for the consequences were too important. And as I had recommended, the consensus was that we should sail south, skirt Smith Island, then make a dash across the Western Bar at Old Inlet. Which we hastened to do, and most successfully I might add, going unnoticed by the Union fleet which concentrated their efforts on Ft. Fisher.

My prayers and those of the crew were for our friend Colonel Lamb who had rescued us on more than one occasion. I pondered his fate and the fate of the fort. If it fell, Wilmington would fall as well, and I wanted to be at home to protect you and Lacey, Mother, if that should occur.

What happened next was most unexpected.

Melanie's lips were parted and her expression was eager. I couldn't see my own face but I knew that I must have appeared as expectant as she. I felt like I knew Thomas Pettigrew as well as I knew any of my friends and the thought of him being taken prisoner filled me with sadness.

"Don't stop," Melanie said.

"You should see your face," I said.

"You should see yours. Hurry. Read."

I read on.

We sailed past Smithville which from the river looked like a ghost town. Not a soul could be seen. The townsfolk had fled for cover. Onward we steamed upriver until we reached Ft. Fisher. The shelling of the fort was of such intensity, the soldiers there were unable to scale the ramparts to man their guns. From the Union ironsides, eleven- and fifteen-inch shells bowled across the earthworks, many striking the river. Then the unthinkable happened. One of the mighty shells crashed into our starboard side. With a fifteen inch hole below the water line, the hull was soon flooding.

The men could not bail fast enough. I called for more steam power, hoping that even with the drag of the water, we might sail far enough up the Cape Fear to make it home.

At Craig's Landing, the Gibraltar began to sink. And to our horror, Union troops awaited us at the Landing. We were transporting four kegs of gold. These could not fall into the hands of the enemy. I asked for volunteers and many heeded the call. They descended into the flooding hull of the ship to enlarge the holes to hasten the sinking of the ship before the Federals could board her. If the Confederacy could not have the gold, the Union would not get it either.

By the time Federal troops rowed out to take us captive, the ship was almost fully under water. We were taken prisoner, led across Federal Point on foot, and from there forced into launch boats and rowed out to Admiral Porter on the USS Malvern. We were not ill-treated on the ship. And eventually we were delivered here to Point Lookout.

I know the war is swiftly coming to an end. I know I will be coming home to your loving faces soon. But, in the event that does not occur, I wanted you to have the information that four kegs of gold lie in the wreckage of the Gibraltar off Craig's Landing. Confide this secret to no one until peace is restored, for in the turbulent days ahead you will not know whom to trust. But wait, Mother, and then when the time is right, take this letter to Jim Billy Craig or Captain Thompson. I trust these men. They will know the proper disposition of the gold, and they will see that you are compensated.

Spring is coming, the nights grow warm. In my dreams I see our garden, the pink azaleas blooming, the dogwoods spreading over the hillside, white as a field of cotton.

May God keep you and Lacey in His care.

 Your loving son,
 Thomas

"Oh, Melanie, what a sad tale. And the note Lacey wrote said, Thomas is dead. Word of his death must have reached

Mrs. Pettigrew and Lacey before this letter got there. That is what I am assuming."

"But why wouldn't they open the letter?" Melanie wanted to know.

"I can only guess that Mrs. Pettigrew was too distraught to be thinking clearly. Or perhaps she was not at home when the letter was delivered. She might have been living with her sister in Robeson County. Perhaps the letter was left with a trusted servant, and then with the chaos of Reconstruction, the influx of the carpet baggers, the turmoil, it was misplaced. And Lacey thought it fitting to have a burial service, you know how kids do that, and she buried her favorite doll as a kind of sacrifice, along with something that had belonged to the Captain — this letter."

Melanie reached over and gave me a hug. "This story breaks my heart. But Ashley, we've got to get going."

"Wait a minute. Now we know what is behind the murders and the theft of Binkie's briefcase and the Captain's journal. Someone knew there was gold at the bottom of the Cape Fear and they'd stop at nothing to find out where it was sunken. Who was it who was talking about gold recently?"

I thought for a moment. "Oh, yes, it was Bo. Remember? Bo said something like if he found gold he would not report it. He'd just take it."

"As much as I hate to say this, we've got to call that dreadful Diane Sherwood again," Melanie said. "But later. Right now we've got an appointment for you to try on your wedding gown."

21

Just as we pulled into the parking lot of the bridal salon, Melanie got a call. She has switched from a hand-held cell phone to one that fits over her ear, very convenient if not a bit reminiscent of "Mork." But hey, I'm getting one too.

"Hello, sweetheart," she said romantically. Cam. "What's my fella up to?"

I could only hear Melanie's side of the conversation but she whispered to me, "Cam and Jon took the *Hot Momma* out for a spin."

I already knew this. It was Saturday after all and Jon deserved a break. He had assured me they would not be diving, only sailing. And that is why I had agreed to meet the carpenter at the Captain's house.

"Where are y'all?" she asked.

"They're down around Ft. Fisher," she murmured to me.

"Tell him about the Captain's letter," I prompted.

"Oh, yes. We've got interesting news, Cam." And she proceeded to recite the contents of the Captain's letter to him over the phone and told him how the Captain had said his ship the *Gibraltar* had sunk off Craig's Landing with gold on board.

I couldn't wait to show the letter to Jon. He was meeting me at my house later that night.

Melanie disconnected with, "Well, bye, sugar. Don't wear yourself out sailing. Save a little bit of yourself for me for tonight."

To me she said, "OK, let's go try on your wedding gown. I have to fly to New York to try on mine, but Vera is not ready for me yet. What a backlog that girl has got."

"Melanie, you are spending a fortune on this wedding. We've got to find time to sit down and review the expenses. I don't want a big ticket wedding. I thought we were going to keep it simple. Wedding in the church, reception at the hunting lodge. Keep the guest list somewhat shy of the entire town."

Melanie got out of the car, slammed the door, and marched off to the bridal salon with me trailing along.

My wedding dress fit like a dream. It was simplicity itself, and did wonders for my figure which, unlike Melanie's, is not perfect. I confess to have a bit of a poochy stomach. But in the gown, I looked like a bride; I felt like a bride. I didn't want to take it off but did so reluctantly and got back into my dirty work clothes.

"Now you can't gain an ounce," Melanie warned as a half hour later we left the bridal salon with the dress packed in its own special bridal gown garment bag. We spread it out on the back seat of the convertible. "No more desserts for you, little sis."

Melanie headed east on Oleander for her neighborhood. We had decided that until I could get my house back in order, we would store the dress in Melanie's guest room closet. I did not want that pure and lovely gown tainted by what I had come to call "the Patsy karma."

Several police cars whizzed by on the opposite side of the median, sirens blaring and lights blazing, and driving like maniacs in the direction of downtown. And in the distance, we heard more sirens. "What's going on?" I asked.

"Well, at least they're headed in the other direction," Melanie said, and turned onto Greenville Loop Road. Melanie lives at the end of Rabbit Run on Sandpiper Cove. Hers is waterfront property, with her own private boat dock, and she owns a bright red speed boat.

It was a little after five and fully daylight, but here in the heavily wooded neighborhood the streets and lawns were shady. The cool shade felt refreshing after driving around in bright sunlight with the top down.

My cell phone rang. The caller was an excited Binkie. I started to tell him about the Captain's letter we'd just found but he was much too hyper and cut me off.

"Ashley, I've made an important discovery. I don't know why I did not make this connection before. Sometimes I think I'm losing it. I've become so forgetful. There it was staring me in the face."

"You are not getting forgetful," I said. "You've just got a lot on your mind, is all. And what was staring you in the face?"

"Some of the final entries in the journal were about Pettigrew taking command of the *Gibraltar*. It had been bought by a small British shipping company for use by a consortium of textile mill owners."

"Yes," I said, "I know that now. He wrote about it in . . ."

I was about to tell him the details of the letter when he cut me off again.

"Well, I just missed the clue. And I'm so exasperated with myself. I never saw it. I was reading aloud to Ruby from the journal and she is the one who spotted the connection. It's Mullins. The dead man at Two Sisters was Hugh Mullins. And one of the owners of the shipping company was named Mullins as well. So that's the clue. It can't be a coincidence.

We think Hugh Mullins was a descendent of the shipping company Mullins. And we think that something having to do with the shipping company caused him to be murdered. But try as I might I cannot find an entry that tells me why."

"I can tell you why," I cried. And I went on to tell him how Captain Pettigrew was transporting gold and other goods to the Confederacy when his ship was sunk and he was taken prisoner.

"Oh, my, I've heard those rumors all of my life but never believed them."

"Binkie," I interjected, "we've been hearing sirens and seeing police cars driving toward downtown. What's going on down there?"

"We've been hearing sirens too," he replied. "We need to turn on the television and see what's happening but we were both so engrossed in our discovery, we wanted to call you first. Whatever is happening, it has something to do with Memorial Bridge. They've stopped traffic on both ends of the bridge. We can see the lines of cars from our window. Hold on a minute."

I said to Melanie as she turned onto her street, "There's trouble on the bridge."

Binkie was back. "Ruby turned on the TV. You'll never believe this. A terrorist has threatened to blow up Memorial Bridge."

"Oh, no! But wait a minute. You said Mullins was one of the shipping company owners. Who were the other owners?"

"There was only one other. Ramsey. Mullins and Ramsey, they were the owners. Ashley, I can't talk. There's a police officer at our door. We're being evacuated."

"Go! Go!" I shouted into the phone. "Be safe." But he was gone.

The plot had thickened and my brain raced feverishly to distil it into something that I could comprehend. Melanie pulled into the driveway in front of her ranch house. "You're awfully quiet over there," she said, interrupting my attempts to weave a scenario out of what I'd just learned.

"Melanie, you'll never believe this. A terrorist has threatened to blow up Memorial Bridge! That's where all those police cars were going. And that is why we've been hearing sirens. But listen to this. This is really odd. The shipping company that owned the *Gibraltar* was named Mullins and Ramsey. Get it! Ramsey. Drew Ramsey! He's involved in this."

Melanie turned to me, eyes wide in horror. "Drew? Drew Ramsey? Our musician? Ashley, Drew is on the *Hot Momma* with Cam and Jon. If he's the one . . . if he's the murderer! We've got to call the boys!"

22

Melanie called Cam and I called Jon.

"Voice mail," she said. "All I get is voice mail."

"Me, too. Jon's not answering."

"Let's try the ship's phone." And we took turns calling the ship, but got the same response. Voice mail. We left frantic messages.

"I have a really bad feeling," I said.

"I'm calling 911," Melanie said. But after several minutes, she just turned to me and wailed, "They're not answering."

"With the threat to the bridge, all 911 lines must be jammed. Binkie said they were evacuating the homes around the bridge."

"Ashley, our men are in peril. It's up to us to save them. Come on."

"Come on where? We'll never get through. Traffic will be jammed up for miles," I protested.

"Not the car. The boat. We'll take the boat."

"Ah! Super idea," I said. "Let's go."

She jumped out of the car and reached for my wedding gown. "I'll get the boat keys and put this inside."

She was gone in a flash and I raced down the path to the boat house. The Coast Guard station was right across Greenville Sound on the south point of Wrightsville Beach. Their cutters must have departed the port in response to the terrorist threat because I didn't see any activity around the dock.

Melanie joined me at the boat house, started up the engine, and within minutes we were motoring out of Hewletts Creek and into the waterway. Her speed boat was a 525 horse power Phantom Fury. At the helm, she cried, "Hang on! This boat can go from 0 to 60 in 20 seconds. I've never tried it before but here she goes." And the sporty red boat cut through the current so fast it took my breath away. By the time we flashed by Money Island, I was wet with spray.

I had to shout to be heard. "Drew Ramsey and Hugh Mullins learned about the sinking of the *Gibraltar* and the vanished gold. Maybe the story was common knowledge in their families, or perhaps they came across old family records that told of the shipment of gold on the *Gibraltar*."

Melanie shouted too. "Somehow they learned of the existence of Captain Pettigrew's journal. They thought the location of the sunken blockade runner would be written about in the journal. They would not have known that the Captain was taken prisoner and conveyed that information in a letter to his mother."

"Which his mother never read," I cried. "No one read the letter. Until now."

"So perhaps Drew doesn't know about the location of the gold," Melanie shouted, as we passed the mouth of Whiskey Creek.

Wishful thinking! "Oh, he knows," I said. "Cam would have been much too excited not to tell."

"Our men are in peril, Ashley! They are on board the *Hot Momma* with a killer. Well, I didn't wait this long to find a man worthy of marriage to lose him to a second-rate musician! So here goes!" And she shoved the throttle forward. The sportster flew down Masonboro Sound.

Snow's Cut is a man-made channel that divides Wilmington from Carolina Beach and connects the Intracoastal Waterway with the Cape Fear basin. We soared through the churning water, sailed under the Carolina Beach bridge, and headed west for the Cape Fear River.

Once in the river, Melanie slowed the engine. The river spread before us, vast and broad. Not a sign of watercraft could be seen. "Where is everyone?" she asked.

"Could the Coast Guard have cleared the river?" I wondered.

"Or they've all sailed to Wilmington toward the bridge. To see what happens next."

She turned to me, her red hair as wet as mine, and I said, "You know, Melanie, I don't think there is a terrorist threat. I think Drew called in a threat to the PD or the Coast Guard station, knowing they'd all race for the bridge . . ."

"Leaving this area clear and unattended, so that he could dive for the gold and sail away with it," she finished.
"Oh, you are a genius, baby sister."

"Sail away on the *Hot Momma*," I said. "With our men!"

"Not if we have anything to say about it," she declared and pushed forward on the throttle.

"But wait a minute, Melanie. Nobody knows where Craig's Landing is actually located. Scholars and historians don't know. They can only guess. They think it was somewhere in the vicinity of where the Air Force Recreational Park is now. Somewhere between Kure Beach and Ft. Fisher."

At this point, the river flowed swiftly in its rush to join the Atlantic. On the western bank stood the grand Orton Plantation. And, I realized with astonishment, Sunny Point.

"I know why he had to resort to the ruse of a terrorist bomb on Memorial Bridge," I said excitedly. "The Sunny Point Army Terminal is directly across the river, and even though it's inactive, there are still army personnel on the base. He couldn't risk being intercepted by them. So if they all rushed north to the bridge, he'd be free to dive for the gold, hoist it on board, and sail away."

Melanie cut the engine. "We've got to be quiet from here on. The chances of him finding that gold are zero. Nobody knows where Craig's Landing used to be, so he won't know either."

"Maybe he thinks he'll get lucky," I said. I had a dreadful thought. "Or maybe he thinks Jon and Cam know where it is and he is forcing them to tell at gun point. We've got to find them. Do you have a plan?"

"Yes. We'll sneak on board the *Hot Momma*, hope he's in the water, and sail her away, leaving him behind."

"But what if Jon and Cam are diving with him? We can't sail off without them. What if they don't know anything about the bogus terrorist plot to blow up Memorial Bridge?"

"Let's just pray they are not diving," she replied, as the Fury floated downstream.

"And let's pray they are still alive," I whispered.

The river was dark and menacing, shaded by the tall trees on the western shore. Far to the South I could see the tip of the Old Baldy Lighthouse.

And then suddenly, there was the *Hot* Momma, directly ahead, anchored off the forested shore. The current was outbound and delivered us to the aft of Cam's sleek white yacht without a whisper of a sound. Melanie steered for the sport deck. I jumped onto the deck, uncoiled the rope and tied it securely to a cleat.

Melanie scrambled onto the sport deck and together we stealthily mounted the outside stairs. Standing on either side of the sliding glass doors, we peered into the salon.

"He's not in there," Melanie said.

"And neither are Jon and Cam," I said.

"Come on," she said, and carefully slid the glass door open. And naturally I followed. Don't I always follow Melanie?

"Shuuussshhh," she hissed unnecessarily. I knew enough not to make noise. Melanie always sees herself as the leader and me as the follower, and most times I accept those roles, but this was different — we were on a mission to save the lives of the men we loved.

I sidled along the paneled wall of the salon. "We've got to search the ship, and we've got to be quiet about it," I mouthed. Thick beige carpeting muffled our footsteps as we made our way to the galley/dining area. We stopped at the large granite-topped island and listened.

I shook my head negatively. I heard nothing more than the creak of the boat in the water, and the soft sound of the current lapping the boat's hull.

I pointed to the steps that led to the bow and the pilot-house. I started up them, not making a sound. Melanie was at my heels.

The sight that met my eyes made me gasp, "No!" but still in a whisper.

"Oh, you poor babies," Melanie cried softly.

Jon and Cam were sitting on the floor, back to back, bound together with duct tape. Their wrists and ankles were bound as well, and tape covered their mouths. But their eyes were alive and alert and happy to see us.

I hurried to Jon. "This might hurt," I said squeamishly. "But I've got to peel off that tape."

Seizing one corner between thumb and forefinger, I pulled off the tape as gently as I could, while Melanie did the same for Cam. "Poor baby," she said again, and kissed Cam's freed lips.

"Thank God, you're here," Jon said. Already Melanie and I were unwinding the duct tape from their torsos. The tape made a sucking sound as it was released.

"Where is he?" I asked. "Where's Drew?"

I freed Jon's hands.

"He's down there," Cam said soberly, nodding with his chin to the river beneath the ship.

The men unwrapped their ankles and got to their feet.

"We've got to get out of here," Melanie said and started for the helm.

"He's gone," Jon said with finality, and rubbed his wrists back to life. And when I looked at him questioningly, he went on to tell me what he and Cam already knew. "He won't be coming up."

"What?" Melanie asked.

But immediately I knew.

"He took my gear," Cam said. "He's about the same size as me so he suited up in my wetsuit."

"And he took Cam's gear. The tank with the slow leak," Jon said.

"What slow leak?" Melanie asked, confused.

Jon went on, "He didn't know enough to check the pressure gauge or the flow-out air. I don't believe he had any experience. But he was willing to take the risk. All he was thinking about was getting to that gold, and spending it."

"I never had the tank repaired," Cam explained. "I was going to but I just didn't get around to it. No one uses that gear but me. I never dreamed anyone would." He looked at his watch and his red, sore wrists. "As he was descending, he'd never notice the bubbles coming from the tank. And when he realized he was out of air, he'd be too deep to swim back up. Plus, he'd probably panic and consume what little air there was left instead of conserving it.

"He's been down there over an hour. He won't be coming up."

23

"We met Drew Ramsey a few years ago at a bikers' meet in Myrtle Beach," Jimmy Pogue said.

As soon as the news had broken that the murderer was Drew Ramsey and that the Coast Guard had recovered his body from the Cape Fear, Jimmy Pogue came out of hiding and returned to Wilmington.

"He'd had too much to drink. We all drank too much at a bike meet. When he found out who Patsy was, that she was a well-known mystery writer, he began telling her the story of the lost gold. He told us that he was the rightful heir because the gold had belonged to his ancestors, had been payment to the Confederacy in exchange for cotton, but as there was no longer a Confederate government, he had every right to it.

"He had records showing that the *Gibraltar* had sailed with gold from Liverpool and had disappeared during the assault on Ft. Fisher. Somehow he was able to learn that Captain Pettigrew and the crew had been taken prisoner, but that the *Gibraltar* went down. He didn't know where. That's when he moved to New York and befriended you, Laura."

We were gathered on my patio on Monday evening, consuming glasses of wicked martinis that Jon had concocted. All of us were glad to be alive. Glad that the ordeal was over.

Laura said, "But he never let on he knew I was a descendent of the Captain's. Instead, he pretended to be interested in the blockade of Wilmington. So I was the one who told him all about the Captain and his adventures as a blockade runner. I even told him there was a journal and that I was sending it to Professor Benjamin Higgins."

"Did you say Drew Ramsey had been a biker?" Clarence Gaston asked. Then he turned to me. "Did you know that it was a motorcycle that struck me on Third Street? The motorcycle shattered my lower spine and left me paralyzed from the waist down. That's why I am in this wheelchair."

"Do you think it was Drew?" I asked.

"Must have been. If it had been a true accident, the person would have stopped. I think it was premeditated. He wanted me out of the way, so he could search the house. Remember, Laura? The police were always saying vandals were breaking in, but it must have been him."

"And he killed Patsy because she recognized him and suspected he had murdered Hugh Mullins," Jimmy said. "She was recording her suspicions on a tape recorder."

"I found the tape in my house, Jimmy," I said. "I turned it over to the police."

"I wanted to go to the police too but Patsy said no. Patsy wasn't afraid of anyone. All the glory she experienced with her first book's awards went to her head. She thought she was God's gift to the literary world. That she could do no wrong. She thought: No one would dare lift a finger to the great Patsy Pogue!"

"She did have a lot of confidence," I said, wanting to be kind to a grieving husband.

"Confidence? She was arrogant. Coasted along on those early awards. Each succeeding book was poorer and poorer. She wouldn't listen to me."

He leaned forward, intent on explaining her, intent on understanding her himself.

"You'd have to see where she came from. How she was raised. Her people were dirt poor. And ignorant? She was the only one with any brains. The only one to go to college. But she never did finish. Quit when she met me. Those were the people she wrote about in her books. She couldn't accept that times and tastes had changed, and that those characters were no longer characters but caricatures."

"I saw you leave that day," I said, "the morning when she was killed. Did you discover that she was dead?"

Jimmy had the decency to hang his head. "I did. She had no pulse. I was a coward. I knew who had killed her and I knew he'd be after me next. So I ran. I hid out with her family in Lincoln County, way out in the country. Her people populate a large rural area there. You can't get up their road without one of them knowing. I knew I'd be safe there."

He managed a dry chuckle. "That's who she was always collecting things for. All the furniture off the street, all the knick knacks. We'd pile them in the truck and drive them up that country road and her folks would be tickled pink."

Everyone has a good side, I thought. And Patsy loved her family.

"But I thought she had money," Melanie said. "She led me to believe she was going to buy a large house."

"She was doing that for me," Jimmy said. "It had been a dream of mine to buy a large house and convert it into a bed and breakfast. I thought it was something we could do together, run the B&B, especially since her career as a writer was over."

"But how did you plan to pay for it?" Melanie asked.

"I think we could have gotten a loan. I'd have taken a job. And I was trying to convince Patsy to find a job too."

"But why did she say you should have burned the house

down?" I asked. "Sorry, I didn't mean to eavesdrop, but I did overhear her say that."

"She didn't mean burn it to the ground, just create some fire damage. Then we could have gotten it cheaper. We were going to have to do a lot of restoration and remodeling anyway. I'm pretty handy with a hammer, and so are many of her brothers. We were going to do most of the work ourselves."

"So you didn't want to buy the Captain's house because you thought gold was hidden inside?" Jon asked. "Care for a refill, Jimmy?"

Jimmy lifted his glass. "No, I wrote a book of my own once. On the fall of Ft. Fisher. So I knew that if Captain Pettigrew had been taken prisoner, he would not have been able to deliver gold to his house and hide it there. I just assumed the Union Army had confiscated it. We wanted the house for its location, the bluff over the river. And for its history. The history of the house would have attracted guests to our B&B."

"Well, that's true," Melanie said.

"The police say they will release her body tomorrow," Jimmy said. "Her people are coming and we are taking her home."

"I'm sorry for your loss," I said.

Cam said, "I know it is not my fault, yet I feel guilty about my leaky air tank. I never dreamed someone would try to use it. No one ever uses my wetsuit or my gear but me."

Melanie slipped an arm around his shoulder. "It is not your fault and I want you to stop blaming yourself."

Cam went on, "That last time we went diving, the Saturday I had a mishap with my air tube, after Jon and I returned to the boat from the medical center, I just laid out my wetsuit on the deck to dry. And I put the tank into one of the lockers, planning to have it checked, never thinking someone would take it."

"Melanie is right, Cam," Jon said. "You couldn't know."

He topped off our glasses, then said. "The moment Cam told Drew about Melanie's phone call and that you had found the Captain's letter that revealed where the gold had been sunken, he became a changed man. Gone were the polite manners, the cool charm. He became driven. Consumed."

"He'd been in a fight," Cam said.

"Bruised, was he?" Binkie asked. "I gave him a beating he'd never forget."

Jon went on, "The excuse he gave was that someone tried to rob him late one night. We just never put it together than he was the one who attacked you, Binkie. Anyway, he had on a big baggy shirt."

"Like the one he had on when he was piloting that speed boat and almost hit your deck?" I said.

"I guess that was him," Jon said. "Under that shirt, he had a gun tucked into his waist band. Who would have thought he was armed? He forced us to tape each other's ankles and wrists and then when we couldn't move, he put the gun back inside his waistband and taped us to each other, back to back. Last, he taped our mouths shut."

"So when he came up to the wheelhouse dressed in my wetsuit, there was no way I could warn him," Cam said.

Jon continued, "He called Wilmington PD, said he was part of a terrorist movement and that he had planted a bomb on Memorial Bridge. Then he tossed the phone overboard. Guess he thought they might use GPS to trace the location of the call.

"He knew enough about sailing to pilot the yacht up the coast to where he thought Craig's Landing used to be located. He said he had memorized the contour of the coast line from old maps and he knew just where to look. After that . . . well, you know the end of the story."

"The end of the story is that Jon and I have gutsy, beautiful women so much in love with us they risked their lives to rescue us," Cam said, and gave Melanie one of his adoring looks.

When the Coast Guard divers went down to recover Drew's body, they reported seeing no evidence of the sunken blockade runner *Gibraltar*. With a hundred and forty-three years of coastal storms, the changing currents could have swept the ship far from its original position. The *Gibraltar* and its cargo of gold would now become the stuff of legends. Divers and scavengers would lust to find it. But the state's Underwater Archeology Department would scan the area with sonar and if any diving team could find the *Gibraltar*, they would.

The next afternoon I was driving west out Highway 74/76 to Leland to meet Melanie at Elaine McDuff's bakery shop to finalize the cake selections. I was playing a CD of the Beatles and singing along to "All You Need is Love" when suddenly something that looked like a large black cloud filled my rearview mirror. I blinked and looked again. The black cloud was approaching rapidly. And then just as rapidly it surrounded me. The noise was deafening, drowning out John and Paul, George and Ringo. Motorcycles, twenty, thirty, and more, flowed around both sides of my car, and behind it and in front of it. The drivers wore black leather jackets and black helmets, and chains. Their ladies, clutching onto the leather clad drivers, were scary looking. And dressed all in black too. They were a tough band, and they didn't like it one bit that I had somehow landed smack dab in the middle of their parade.

With looks that could kill, they motioned me over to the side of the road, or gave me the Greek salute or shook their fists at me. But I couldn't pull over to the curb to let them pass, because my right side was blocked by motorcycles zooming past me.

They were going around me and I could only hope they'd soon out-distance me and be gone. I slowed down. I didn't want to be in their parade any more than they wanted me there.

There must have been a hundred of them. And then the truck appeared. A white pickup with an open back. At that point, a space magically opened up on my right and I pulled over to the curb and stopped. The driver of the white truck waved to me as he drove by.

Jimmy. It was Jimmy Pogue. In the truck's bed rested a shiny new coffin with fancy hardware. Draped with the Confederate flag.

I could feel my eyes bulging wide. Patsy's coffin. Jimmy had said her people were coming to take her home. She was on her way to her final resting place in Lincoln County.

Wait until I tell Melanie, I kept thinking as I re-entered the highway and continued my journey to Leland.
In Elaine's parking lot, I waited in my car until Melanie pulled in beside me. "Did you see them?" I shouted.

"See who?" she asked.

And I told her all about Patsy's most unorthodox funeral procession.

Melanie just arched her eyebrows and gave her hair a swing. "Takes all kinds." She had already moved on from the Patsy murder and was focusing on our wedding. "OK, now I don't want to hear any arguments from you. I've decided on the five tier wedding cake, vanilla and chocolate layers with fondant icing."

"Fondant, but isn't that the most . . . "

Melanie glowered at me. "Yes, it's the most expensive but it's the classiest and has the smooth matte finish that is so perfect for decorations. Like a cascade of sugar fruits, you know, pears and cherries, so Christmassy looking. For the bachelor's cake, I think . . ."

She turned on me so abruptly I almost bumped into her.

"Oh, oh," she cried, "I almost forgot," and she actually did a little jump into the air and twirled around, like from her high school cheer leader's days — all she needed were pompoms. "The most exciting thing has happened. Colin Cowie is available. He's going to come down here and plan everything for us."

"What?"

"Oh, don't look so blank. Even you know who Colin Cowie is. He planned Oprah's fiftieth birthday party. He is the best party and wedding planner, and so hard to get. But Candy gave him a call for me!"

"Melanie! I thought we agreed we were going to keep this simple. You are spending a fortune on this wedding and we . . ."

"I declare, Ashley, what do you think money is for? We're alive for pity sakes. You can't take it with you. Besides I owe you for what I put you through with Patsy."

She gave me a wicked grin. "And as Patsy Pogue would say: Hearses don't come with no luggage racks!"

Coming Chritsmas 2007

CHRISTMAS WEDDING

As Ashley and Melanie prepare to walk down the aisle, a most surprising wedding crasher threatens to delay the wedding — indefinitely!

Orange Coconut Cookies

This easy, fool proof recipe was created by Dennis Madsen, innkeeper and chef, The Verandas Bed & Breakfast, www.verandas.com
Ingredients:
1 box Duncan Hines Orange Supreme Cake Mix, divided
2 eggs
1/4 cup white sugar
1/2 cup vegetable oil
1 cup sweetened coconut, divided

In the bowl of your mixer,
Mix eggs, oil, and sugar.

Add 1/2 box dry cake mix. Mix well.
Add 1/2 cup coconut. Mix.

Drop on cookie sheet. Dennis uses a #70 cookie scoop, about 1 T.

Bake for 12 minutes at 365 degrees.

Cool on wire rack.

Eat as soon as cool.

Makes about 3 1/2 dozen cookies.

ENJOY!

ORDER FORM

Your name: _____

Your shipping address: _____

City:_____State:_____Zip:_____

email address: _____

Please indicate your choices:

____ MURDER ON THE CANDLELIGHT TOUR ($15)

____ MURDER AT THE AZALEA FESTIVAL ($15)

____ MURDER ON THE GHOST WALK ($15)

____ MURDER AT WRIGHTSVILLE BEACH ($15)

____ MURDER ON THE ICW ($15)

____ MURDER ON THE CAPE FEAR ($15)

Coming December 2007, CHRISTMAS WEDDING $15

Take any two books for $25, three books for $40,
four books for $50, five for $60, six for $75.

Add shipping:
1 book = $2.50		4 books = $5.00
2 books = $3.50		5 books = $6.00
3 books = $4.50		6 books = $7.00

Total Enclosed: $_____

Make check payable and mail to:
Ellen Hunter • PO Box 38041
Greensboro, NC 27438

Please allow 30 days for receipt. Books are shipped by media mail.

THANK YOU!